ENJc

Charlie TAYLOR
,

'WMD' the Bikini Project

During the first few months of 2003 a coalition of armed forces invaded Iraq in an operation entitled 'Iraqi Freedom'. Among the justifications given for this action was the following; 'To locate and destroy Iraqi Weapons of Mass Destruction'… To date none have been found!

Now in 2016 there is a new coalition and WMD's are again on the agenda; … but this is a secret that must never be revealed!

One ordinary man though, has stumbled upon the secret … and it could start wars and kill thousands!

However, this has put him in mortal danger, as the governments involved will stop at nothing to silence him … Theirs is a deadly game to be played out on Spain's Costa del Sol.

He must find a way to fight back … or die!

Charlie Taylor

'If you're going through hell, keep going' … Winston Churchill

Dedicated to my grandchildren Charlie and Taylor who inspired me to write this book,

also

to John, whom I met in Kos … the real Frankie

charlietaylor2397@gmail.com

amazon.com/author/taylorcharlie2019

Tuesday 26th April 2016 … 11.00am

Three Wise Men!

On a very warm Spring day, under a cloudless blue sky, Georgio, the duty manager of the luxurious **Parador Hotel** in **Nerja, Spain,** watched, as five men climbed out of the air-conditioned comfort of a black 4 x 4, walked up the six marble steps and entered the hotel. Two of the men, in matching white shirts and sunglasses, rejected the first suite offered and demanded another random one, with unoccupied rooms on either side. Whilst Mr Disney, Mr Drayton-Manor and Mr Zawraa signed the hotel register, the two 'shirts' scanned all three rooms for electronic listening devices and locked rooms 102 and 106. One then remained to guard the chosen room, as the second went down to the foyer to collect the three VIP's and escort them up to room 104. The two similarly attired men, then returned to their vehicle and closely monitored anyone entering or exiting the hotel.

They were satisfied that every possible precaution had been taken!

Georgio, already curious by his guest's behaviour, read the hotel register and became further intrigued. He'd spent seven years working in a hotel in Birmingham, England and immediately recognized the name 'Drayton-Manor' as that of a well-known British theme park. Like everyone else he also knew the name 'Disney' as arguably the world's most famous theme park, and Zawraa? who knows? but he'd hazard a guess.

Fate stirred!

It was almost five hours later, as he was viewing the hotel's CCTV system, that he saw the three men emerge from their meeting and make their way to the foyer.

After several minutes of polite conversation, during which one of them visited the men's room, all three were then collected by the two men in white shirts and escorted to the waiting black BMW X5. All five men then set off for their return journey to Malaga airport.

The three 'names' were certain, that the agenda they had discussed, was known only to a few selected persons in the world. It was absolutely vital it should stay that way. However, behind them, on a small table adjacent to the *gent's* restroom, lay a forgotten black leather document folder

Fate was awake!

Two hours later, having retrieved the folder and with the well-intentioned purpose of tracing its owner, Georgio made the first of three fatal errors … *he opened it!*

He read the first few pages of a long document entitled **'The Bikini Project'** and his curiosity got the better of him.

He now made the second fatal error … *he decided to show the contents to a friend!*

The third and final fatal error … was to play back the CCTV footage of the men's arrival and departure and using his mobile phone, *record what was on the monitor*. He also began photographing the documents themselves!

He little realised that these three irreversible actions, would cost him his life and set off a chain of events, that could result in the death of innocents and a war of nations.

He'd just photographed the seventh page, when too late; he noticed the man in a white shirt and sunglasses, standing at the office doorway. The man's right arm was hanging down by his side and he could just see that the hand was gripping something black.

Only part of that 'something' was visible; but it was unmistakably the handgrip and trigger guard of a small automatic pistol.

Confused and scared, Georgio, mobile phone in hand, pushed past the man and ran out of the hotel towards the town and safety. Sensing a black 4 x 4 moving behind him, he turned left towards the small restaurant called Quixote's and his friend Sergio.

It was there that fate threw him into contact with the angry Englishman!

***

Day 1 … Tuesday 26th April 2016 … 16.42 pm

Stranger in Paradise!

Martin Lamb, had lived in his own private hell long enough. No one would talk to him, his moods had become dark and ugly, almost violent, so why should they? Drink fed the demons within, surfacing only to rage at the innocents around him!

Mary had died walking beside him, the car coming from behind, noisily, deadly, the young driver showing off the new 'toy' to his pals. She'd been nearest the road, plucked from his grasp and taken away, forever! The authorities had called it an accident but to him it felt like murder and now aged 58 he was alone and angry.

That had been seven months ago. He was now in Spain seeking refuge from his torments, hoping that the memories of past holidays would give him solace in his darkest hours. It hadn't been an easy decision to come to Nerja, she'd booked this trip three month before 'it' the accident. They'd planned to look for a property, live out here, where they'd laughed the most, walked and talked the most.

Anger rose in his chest and he tried hard to suppress it. Sitting at Quixote's bar with alcohol tainting his senses, he took another gulp of his large Magno brandy and fought the rage down to a drunken truce.

Twelve hours ago, he'd woken up in a cold overcast Wigan determined to catch the mid-morning flight. He'd stuffed what few possessions he needed; shaving gear, underwear and a couple of T shirts, into a lightweight bag and waited for the taxi taking him to John Lennon airport. Once there he'd tried to follow their usual pattern; all=day breakfast and a pint of Amstel at Weatherspoon's, before going down to the Estuary bar and restaurant for another pint, prior to boarding the Ryanair flight to Malaga. This time though, he'd also downed a Scotch to blank out the voices tormenting him, if he could just make tomorrow!

He hadn't told his family he was leaving, there was no point. They were better off without him, they had their settled lives, they didn't need the poison in his. Now he was sweaty and unkempt, with two days of stubble on his face. Dark patches of damp showed beneath his armpits and he probably smelled foul. He didn't give a damn, as long as the beer was cold and the brandy cheap, so what!

It was going to be a long night!

Although in his late 50's, he was reasonably fit. Whilst he never minded physical labour, he scoffed at those who paid for exercise programs and diets.

After a decade in the British army, he'd spent several years working in the middle east as a technical advisor with the Imperial Iranian army. That is, until its interruption by the 1979 revolution. Following that, any civilian job in the UK was always going to be difficult to settle into. They lacked the complicated formulae of excitement combined with a fixed regime. He'd been a mechanic, coach driver and chauffeur, but like many ex-service personnel before him, it was in a security role that he'd felt the most comfortable.

He'd moved through the industry from armoured cash van driver to the job of retail security guard, eventually attaining the role of 'Business Crime Co-ordinator'. This involved working with various civilian agencies, gathering and sharing intelligence on indigenous and foreign shoplifting teams. These would travel the UK, committing ever more sophisticated thefts and frauds.

Whilst it hadn't been a glamorous lifestyle, it had been a good one, with just enough excitement to keep him alert, and Mary had been supportive throughout. Flash cars and designer labels bored him, Volvo and 'George by Asda' were his style, good beer, average wine and any brandy were his forte. He was grey haired, 'platinum' he called it, whilst Mary would joke 'more like a white rat than the woolly lamb' his name suggested. At 5-foot 10inches tall, he also had the inevitable slight paunch, due mainly to the recent poor diet and alcohol. She used to say he had a distinguished look, chiselled verging on rugged, only now he looked tired and pissed. What once had been generous humour, had since been replaced with short intolerance. He didn't waste pointless smiles. Where previously he'd been a quiet man, with an even temperament, now he'd blow up at fools of any kind. He'd always tried to do his best for Mary and the kids, but he changed after 'it' now his only ambition was release or revenge.

They'd been to Nerja many times, it was on the Costa del Sol, fifty kilometres east of Malaga. Formerly a sleepy fishing village, set between the mountainous Sierras and the craggy shoreline of the Mediterranean. It had quaint cobbled streets and whitewashed houses of the 'old town' plus pretty beaches in the many steep rocky coves. In recent times it had evolved into a popular tourist destination. The town's progress into the commercial world was confirmed, by the numerous colourful scooters, delivering goods and personnel as they buzzed to and fro like human bees.

Adjacent to the church and defined by two rows of palm trees, was the famous Balcon de Europa, built out onto a rocky outcrop like a giant marble pier. The local bars and restaurants, dotted throughout the town, were famous for dispensing friendliness and tapas in equally generous portions. With a large ex-pat community, consisting mostly of retirees, anyone hoping to enjoy drunken revelry would be better off travelling to the more westerly locations like Fuengerola, or Benalmadena. In Nerja, serenity, calm and gentle humour were the order of the day.

Each time as soon as they'd arrived, they would dump the cases in the apartment on Calle Los Huertos and visit Sevillano's for pre-dinner drinks. Then they'd seek out Sergio, who owned Quixote's, their favourite café/bar. It was on Plaza del Olvido, a small square between Calle Los Huertos and Calle Frigliana. There, they'd have freshly grilled sardines, washed down with glasses of Rioja wine and local Brandy, 'to get into the holiday mood'. Then they'd tipsily return to the apartment; to unpack and get changed, ready for a late night of fun and 'tapas' in the old Spanish quarter, still laughing at Sergio's comical attempts at telling jokes in English.

They'd always try and time their holidays to coincide with the 'Tapas tour', spending the week trying to get as many stamps on the 'Tapas passport' as time and intoxication permitted. They also favoured the San Isidro celebrations, when farmers and townsfolk, all quaffing copious amounts of beer and

Sangria, would parade highly decorated floats and carts through the town. These would be towed by tassel adorned horses, mules, tractors or even cattle. Another of their traditional outings would be a Sunday afternoon down at the Boatyard'. There amongst the many small motor boats and dinghies, they'd eat Sunday lunch, drink beer and wine whilst singing along with the 'Flying Dolphins and Charlie Miller' a superb group of local musicians. On the way back it was traditional to call in at Hemmingway's or Bar 19 for a Gin and Tonic or cocktail.

Pictures of those halcyon days, formed like some masochistic torture, feeding both exquisite pleasure and bottomless depression, to his silently screaming mind.

Sergio, a widower himself, had become a close friend. His was a typically Spanish bar, made popular by reputation and perfectly summed up the local way of life. Mid-morning, the women would meet, after getting the kids off to school and doing the laundry. They'd share strong creamy coffee, cigarettes and gossip, before doing the shopping and returning home to prepare the evening meal. At lunch time, the old men of the town would meet to smoke pungent cigarettes whilst drinking Cruzcampo beer or brandy and discuss fishing trips of old. Politics and other controversial subjects were taboo … stress wasn't on the agenda! Finally, late afternoon and into the night, tourists and local families would come, to share the day's events and bathe in each other's company.

A hand on his shoulder dragged him back from the personal hell he called memories. Looking up he saw the concerned features of his friend 'I'm sorry Sergio I didn't mean it to be like this maybe I shouldn't have come'

'But you did come my friend, and it is good you come, it is important for you yes!' it wasn't a question 'She lovely lady we drink to her!'

Lamb sat outside, on one of the many cheap plastic chairs and stared at the unsteady table in front of him. Ignoring the hot burning sun on his back he remembered their last visit. picturing her opposite then took a swallow of the extra-large Brandy Sergio had poured. He was determined not to turn into a sympathy seeking drunk, it wasn't what she'd have wanted, drunk she'd tolerate, sympathy seeking? ... definitely not!

'Yes, and I'll have the sardines please amigo' she'd always stressed it was important he ate plenty of fish 'Sergio thank you, the brandy is good, and after my meal we should share another'.

'Of course, my friend we sit and talk, make happy memories yes, first I fetch some fresh sardines then I cook for you'

It was as he was sitting on the sun-drenched terrace waiting for his food that the stranger appeared, and he looked terrified!

Fate was attention seeking!

He'd appeared off Calle Los Huertos and turned into Calle Frigliana, Lamb gauged him to be Spanish and in his early 60's. He was wearing a white shirt, with a black tie and waistcoat, and he was constantly glancing back. He seemed unsure whether to walk or run and the knuckles on his right hand were white from gripping a mobile phone.

He went into the Café but came straight out again, impatient and agitated! 'Sergio' he said, panic in his voice 'Sergio *donde?* where?'

Shaken out of his thoughts and irritable, Lamb put down his brandy and eyed the man warily 'Don't know, he was here a moment ago, maybe he's just popped out'

For a split second the man glared at the Englishman and then snapped his head round, looking back towards the direction he'd just come from, fear showing in his eyes. Opposite, a deliveryman wheeling crates of 'Coca Cola' on a sack truck stopped, alerted by the tone of the man's voice. The man shot him a pleading glance, then started towards the bar again, just as a vehicle rounded the corner behind him.

The black BMW X5 slowly turning into the street from Calle Los Huertos, looked out of place in the narrow streets of the old town. It had blacked out side windows and the body language of its occupants marked it as different. Two males one older than the other, both wearing identical white short sleeved shirts and sunglasses and both seemingly scanning the alleyways and bars.

And they scared the man.

Dropping the phone on the table he moved away from the cafe and ran down Calle Frigliana, looking back with those same haunted eyes. He tripped and landed on all fours ... then regained his footing and disappeared down the hill. Towards the cliffs above Playa Carabeo!

The X5 continued past the cafe and the passenger looked directly at the Englishman wearing the Liverpool shirt and said something to his companion.

A few seconds later Sergio appeared 'Was someone here, only I hear a voice as I was coming in the back door, it sounded like Georgio an amigo, he the manager from the Parador hotel he sometimes comes here'

'Yes, there was a man here asking for you, and he was acting very strange but he shot off'

Sergio paused and smiled 'He come back soon maybe'

'Probably, but whoever it was he looked very scared'

'I cook the sardines now" Sergio smiled 'Then we talk' he turned and went into the cafe.

It was then that Lamb noticed the dropped Samsung mobile. He picked it up and curious to know what had scared the man so much, walked down the hill to see if he was still nearby. He was almost at the bottom where it joined Calle Carabeo, when he heard the scream.

Fate stretched and took an interest!

Looking around the corner in the direction of the scream, he saw the older of the 'shirts' peering over the balustrade, down at the rocks forty feet below. The X5 was parked on the road with both front doors open.

Twenty feet away a British tourist hugged her companion, calming her, absorbing the sobs. 'Bastards' she yelled 'That was deliberate you bastards!'

The younger of the two shirts looked up at her, his blue eyes burning their way into her nightmares. The older man was speaking into his mobile phone … of the two men he appeared the calmest.

Staying back against the wall, just out of sight whilst not sure why, Lamb was puzzled to see the first man collecting items from the footpath. He was near the balustrade and looking around as only a person with guilt to hide would do. After pocketing the objects, he then manoeuvred the X5 nearer to the kerb and closed the doors.

Spotting Lamb and feeling safer, the English woman was yelling 'I saw it! I saw them push him! He didn't stand a chance, those bastards mugged him and pushed him over the cliff!' Her companion gripped her tighter, hushing her whilst leading her away, not wanting to be part of the horror unfolding around them.

The sirens got louder as the ambulance approached.

Alerted to his presence by the woman, the younger shirt' spotted Lamb standing near the corner and ignoring the hysterical woman, approached him. 'You! he spoke to you! I saw him, what did he say?' His eyes were deep blue and icy cold, and he spoke with an east European accent, the tone of his voice demanding, not questioning and it pissed Lamb off! 'I was speaking to you!' again the attitude.

Lamb looked straight at him 'Ok clown, who spoke to me?' then leaning closer he hissed 'Bin the soddin attitude idiot'

Brushing past the 'attitude' Lamb walked over towards the older shirt at the balustrade and looked down at a twisted body on the rocks. The stranger was lying face up, blood seeping from his head. His twisted legs pointing towards the cliff his head towards the sea. To Lamb it suggested he'd gone over backwards. If he'd jumped, he'd be face down, and even if he'd somersaulted which was unlikely from that height, surely his head would then be nearest the cliff? What was also unusual were his pockets, they were turned inside out. Lamb looked at the older shirt 'You two been giving flying lessons?'

Blue eyes approached and studied him for a second, weighing him up, teetering on the edge of violence. But something cautioned him, this stranger wasn't your average tourist. He lowered his attitude a couple of notches and walked across towards the women 'You go! go now!' then seeing them start to leave he turned his attention back to Lamb 'Ignore her she's how you say … crazy? it was suicide, he was determined to jump over the cliff, we tried to save him and as you can hear we've called the emergency services' he looked down at the Samsung still in Lamb's hand. 'Did he give you anything; a phone maybe?'

The brandy and beer were taking their toll on Lamb and he needed a piss, and anyway from what he had seen he'd rather believe the woman than blue eyes. The shirt was now staring at him unblinking, trying to intimidate him 'This is not something you should get involved in, it could have serious consequences'

Lamb took a deep breath, leaned forward and exhaled into the man's face, his breath foul with the stench of brandy, beer and a long day's travelling, he smiled as blue eyes recoiled 'Sod off!' He walked to the balustrade again, rattled but holding it together for now! Then seeing both shirts distracted by the arrival of the ambulance, he slid the stranger's phone into the barrel of the ancient rusty cannon, ornamented on a plinth close by. If they wanted it, they could whistle Dixie. He leaned over to have another look at the body and as he did so felt a hand on his arm and turned to see the older shirt.

The man spoke to him quietly, attempting to soothe the anger 'I am sorry, my friend is upset, the incident you know I'm sure you understand' he smiled 'Let me introduce myself, I'm Edward Warling and my younger companion here is Filip Wojtek … and you are?

'Gerrard, Stevie Gerrard' Lamb said giving him the same insincere smile 'And yes you've probably guessed it the address is Anfield' with that he turned to leave.

The hand gripped his arm tighter stopping him 'Mr Gerrard' this time a wry smile 'No doubt my companion tried to explain the seriousness of our business, it reaches right up to the highest level I can assure you' he let this sink in 'We could of course tell the local police you have the man's phone, it might prove awkward'

Lamb wrenched the hand from his arm 'Listen I don't give a damn who you are, but tell the police? Go ahead! and if you like I'll fetch the women who witnessed what happened here, they're not too far away' as the smile left the man's face Lamb continued 'The way I see it by making threats your idiot pal has raised more questions than answers' he was getting into his stride now 'He said the man jumped but it just looks a tiny bit suspicious the way he's lying, especially with his pockets turned out'

Now staring at Lamb again, Warling lowered his voice, his mouth firming 'We could say you did it, you mugged him and stole his phone and that he fell trying to escape from you' the last part was hissed impatiently 'Far better to give us what we want now, we know you have it, then we'll all be on our way'

Lamb laughed 'You could say I did it, but it won't get you this imaginary phone you're banging on about, and listen carefully, even if I did have anything, you pair certainly wouldn't be getting it, is that clear? now grab your puppy and piss off!' he paused to make sure both shirts were paying attention

Wojtek made a move towards him but was stopped by the older shirt.

Lamb continued 'Seems to me you've got too many dodgy questions you'll need to answer already' he smiled sarcastically 'I reckon the police would be very interested to know how the man's other possessions ended up in this idiot's pockets' he nodded towards blue eyes 'And they'd certainly raise their eyebrows if you asked them for his phone, you know what, it seems I won't need to fetch the women after all'

The older man again gripped Lamb's shoulder, then stopped with a puzzled expression

'Martin there you are; your sardines they are ready' Sergio strode towards them a serious but calm look on his face. He stretched out an arm and removed the hand gripping his friend's shoulder. 'He has had a long day maybe you talk to him tomorrow yes' with that he started to guide Lamb away.

The second shirt gave that insincere smile again and walked round to face Lamb 'You might think you are being clever but you have no idea what it is you are dealing with, honestly you don't. We will talk again, and you will help us, but for now eat your sardines, ok Martin!' with that both shirts walked over towards the police car pulling into to the kerb.

Lamb paused for a second to see if he was being mentioned then nodded to his friend and together, they walked towards to the café. 'I'll explain over a brandy my friend, although I'm not too sure what happened myself yet' It didn't bother him that he'd not given them the phone, nor was it any business of his why they wanted it. Ok he wasn't entirely comfortable that they might have killed someone for it, but he had his own issues, let them get on with theirs. Blue eyes though, had aggravated the hell out of him and the older guy hadn't been much better, so he certainly wasn't going to be intimidated by them, it could stay where it was!

Fate would have other ideas!

Following his meal, Lamb told Sergio everything he'd seen and heard. His friend had been shocked at the thought Georgio would have committed suicide.

'He was a good catholic man, a widower with grandchildren he would not do this thing!'

Lamb had deliberately not mentioned the mobile phone, there was no point adding worry to his friend's upset. Lack of sleep and excess alcohol finally caught up with him, so they agreed to discuss the recent events and whether they should involve the police, the following day.

***

The shirts came to Quixote's some two hours after Lamb had left, just as Sergio was locking up for the night. They appeared silently, surprising him. Pushing him hard against the wall, blue eyes forcibly gripped Sergio's arm and pushed him back into the café locking the door behind them. Although initially alarmed he didn't resist as there was no point, after all he knew very little. They asked him about his friend, the Englishman; his full name and where he was staying 'Where was he now? What did he know about Georgio's phone? Had Georgio or his Liverpool friend told him anything?' He related what Martin had said, but other than that he couldn't help them, He answered with ease, it even amused him, he knew nothing of any phone, why should he? There were no verbal threats but he sensed a sinister menace in their voices, the younger of the two was certainly on edge. Blue eyes disappeared into the back room and Sergio could faintly hear running water.

The older shirt calmly reassured him 'Ignore the water, it is my friend's obsession with cleanliness'

When blue eyes returned drying his hands, they requested Sergio first give them his mobile phone and secondly to take off his sandals 'Please don't resist it is unnecessary, we are not going to hurt you, this is just a precaution in case you try to contact the Englishman' he continued 'We are going to lock you in the store room purely to give us time to follow up this visit and we will of course notify someone of your whereabouts, also we may want to question you further, this is after all an inter-governmental enquiry'

They bundled Sergio towards the dark store room, pushed him in and closed the door. The floor was wet and he inwardly laughed at the man's stupid habit 'Like a child' he muttered to himself and reached for the light switch.

Elsewhere on Plaza del Olvida the lights dimmed.

***

Edmond Warling looked affectionately at his blue-eyed companion sitting in the X5's driver's seat, and listened to the inevitable rant. The total opposite of himself, the 28-year-old was impatient and predictably wanted to pursue the Englishman immediately. It was his nature and in various other situations, that could be useful.

'Why aren't we going after the Englishman now? I'll feed him his sardines; in fact, I'll ram them down his throat! Who does he think he is?' Warling smiled at the irony of what his angry companion had said 'The man tried to make a fool of me and no one does that to Filip Wojtek and gets away with it!

It had been like that since his childhood in Croatia. Born 'Josip Babic' to wealthy parents, for years he'd watched his drunken mother batter his father to a bloodied mess. In his eyes this made his father a weakling and the longer the beatings went on the more he despised him for not defending himself! As young as ten years old he had sworn an oath, that one day he himself would exact revenge upon his mother. Until then though, he would wait but not forget! Eventually he lost all feelings towards either of his parents, and was glad when they sent him to a top boarding school in Surrey, England.

One day, two years after his arrival, the headmaster called him in to the office, his mother was there to tell him some sad news. She seemed to take pleasure in describing in detail how his father had gone to the nearby railway line and walked calmly towards the hurtling express, arms out wide as if in welcome.

Josip became more withdrawn, a loner who made no friends and disliked authority. He wouldn't complain or sulk, instead, he would wait, plotting until the time was right, then the object of his anger would be made to suffer. The other pupils feared him, and he was the subject of many complaints. His father though had been a major contributor to the school funds, and it was only after the most serious incident that they dared to remove him.

Two days after his Seventeenth birthday, an elderly and senior master Mr Bertram had crossed him. It was late at night, and Josip was discovered in a store room, forcing whiskey down the throat of one of his adversaries, in an attempt to get him expelled for being drunk! Normally he would have made sure no one else witnessed his evil deeds. This time however, the teacher had stumbled across the scene whilst returning a repaired violin to a pupil who urgently needed it for an exam. Mr Bertram had questioned him, demanding he hand over the alcohol, threatening to tell the head in the morning. Josip sneered, mocking the master as he tore down the now drunken pupil's trousers. Then throwing whiskey over the tutor he rushed him and using strength born of fury ripped the man's shirt. Forcing his way past the pair, he slammed the store room door shut whilst screaming accusations, waking everyone in the building.

Welcome to Babic hell!

His mother passed away six months following this incident, and the school were relieved to find him a place on a four-year MA course at the University of Edinburgh. There he studied Russian language and Culture. His vitriol remained however and again the lecturers and students were afraid of his mood swings.

27

Being a loner suited Josip Babic, any relationship he had during this period was merely for his own gratification. often leaving those men or women he encountered, with sleepless nights, fearful of his return. Apart from a debauched two-year gap, he did however study hard. So, it was no surprise, that following several visits to Russia and other soviet speaking countries, he came to the notice of the British intelligence agencies. They could imagine various ways in which his Croatian' credentials could come in handy.

But it was as a 26-year old that they finally saw his real potential. He'd viciously put a UK minister's son in a coma after the young man had scoffed at him by calling him a 'jumped up third world gipsy'. Calls were made, and they found the perfect job for him in 'Core Logistical Analytics (CLA)' a very secretive department, whose head of station was now using the new alias of 'Mr Pontin' ... CLA was known only to twenty-one other people in the world.

They gave Babic a British passport under a new name and 'Filip Wojtek' was born!

*** *** ***

Day 2 ... Wednesday 27th April 2016

Killing Time!

Next morning Lamb awoke late, he was on top of the bed and still in the same clothes he'd arrived in the day before. The events of yesterday were vague in his booze sodden brain and it was only when he looked at the bedside table and saw his own mobile, that very slowly the memories crawled back. His mouth tasted foul, his eyes stung and he smelled of rancid booze and stale sweat.

By now, the time was getting close to 11am, he felt rough and desperately in need of a drink. It was Wednesday and Quixote's wouldn't open until 4pm, so he decided to go to the 'Rack & Ruin' a Bohemian style establishment modelled on the post war bars of Bucharest. It was on Calle Los Huertos, just a short walk from the apartment, and was spotlessly clean, friendly, and the food was good. Rinsing his face in cold water but not changing, he made his way unsteadily outside.

Some two hours later, feeling better, having drunk three bottles of Mahou beer and eaten 'homemade steak pie and chips' he returned to the apartment. The travelling, drink and events took their toll. and again, he slept, images of Mary haunting him into drunken oblivion.

Lamb re-awoke around 5pm feeling almost human. He showered to get rid of the smell of alcohol then changed into his usual sports shirt and beige slacks. The previous day's events seemed surreal but he found he couldn't so easily dismiss the man's death, he needed thinking time. When he'd taken in some rays and balanced his levels of caffeine, alcohol, and calories, maybe he'd find a simple explanation, but somehow, he doubted it. Putting on his RayBan's against the bright sunlight, Lamb made his way around the corner to Quixote's and was alarmed to find it shut, the blinds were down and an official looking notice was taped to the door. It was typed in Spanish and with bile forming in his throat he tried to read it;

'El propietario de este restaurant ha muerto por lo que permanecera cerrado a la espera de un inquirey'

La Policia'

He didn't need a translator, two words stood out *'propietario'* 'owner' and *'muerto'* 'dead'

He staggered away, questions and anger blocking rational thought from his mind. Two streets away he threw up and sobs formed deep in his soul to exit as rage against pointless gods and death. Spittle vomit and tears ran down his chin as he kneeled at the kerbside and passers-by fearfully crossed over to avoid the 'drunken Englishman'

Instinct told him that Sergio's death had to be related to the events of yesterday. Also, out of the depths of his alcohol fuelled despair and anger, he figured the man's mobile phone was somehow at the centre of what had happened. He needed to retrieve it, not only might it give him the reason for his friend's death, but also the identity of the murderers. It could also give him the means for revenge! Another thing crossed his mind, his own life could now be in danger!

Fate shook the dice!

Not only did he have another shower, but he also changed out of his vomit stained clothes, which he binned. Afterwards, he walked down to the cliff top to where ribbons of blue and white tape cordoned off part of the balustrade. Cautiously, watching for both the police and the shirts, he retrieved the phone from the cannon and returned to the apartment.

Deliberately taking his time so as to lower his emotions down to a manageable level, he did a quick check of the phone's contents. They showed various text messages in Spanish which he couldn't understand and likewise the e-mails. But it was the photos and videos which intrigued him, so he removed the memory card and inserted it into his own Blackberry,

Eventually he left the apartment and driven by instinct rather than reason he made his way back to R & R. At the first bin he wiped clean and dumped the man's Samsung, tormented and furious he needed answers. He didn't doubt they had killed his friend; he also knew that somehow violence would descend upon those responsible, he had nothing else to lose! Once inside the bar he climbed onto a stool and ordered a large Soberano brandy. Alison served him so when she passed him his drink, he engaged her in conversation.

'I've just been to Quixote's and there's a notice saying the owner is dead, know anything about it?'

Ali eyed him curiously, his mood had changed since earlier 'You mean Sergio, don't you? I've heard there was some sort of accident but no details, why, did you know him?'

'I've drank there quite a few times; he was a friend and a really nice guy'

'I'm so sorry, he was a lovely bloke, it's such a pity'

Lamb ordered a second brandy and when it came, poured both into one glass, he didn't want disturbing. He then went to the back of the bar and onto the veranda that overlooked Nerja's main car park. The early evening was cool, and he could just discern the faint aroma of the many purple Bugavilla bushes that covered the walls surrounding the car park.

This was a huge square, with one main vehicle entrance and exit, and three small pedestrian alleyways leading off from each of the other sides. It was lit by several tall wooden lamp posts that cast a soft orange glow over the rough dusty surface. He chose the table in the darkest corner figuring that anyone coming in the bar from bright sunlight or street light would be temporarily blinded, giving him a small advantage.

Although it would never have occurred to him before, this seemed the perfect place to try and make sense of the hell around him. The bar had a main front door off the one-way street, it was also only a single lane so no parking was permitted. There was also a rear entrance leading down some lesser known steps to the carpark and that gave him two options for moving, should he need to. Also, he figured that the shirts were almost certainly strangers to the town and with Nerja being notorious for inadequate street parking the chances of them using the main car park were high. It also meant the chances of him seeing them first were equally high.

Lamb switched on his Blackberry, then tapped into the free Wi-Fi and examined the transferred contents. They consisted of three videos and thirty-four photos, each seemingly taken with the mobile phone. The majority of photos appeared to show members of a family but the most recent were unusual, one was of a finger pointing to three names from what appeared to be a page from a hotel registry.

A further seven photos showed typewritten pages and the last was a blurred image that appeared to be an accidental shot.

The first video was shaky footage of two small children both girls around 6 years old, they were playing in the street laughing and running up to the camera and pulling faces, the stranger's grandchildren perhaps?

The second video showed unsteady and grainy pictures of a CCTV monitor, it was of three dark suited men presumably the 'names' being guided through a hotel corridor and entering a room, each was carrying a black leather document holder. Escorting them were two other men.

Both wore white short sleeved shirts and sunglasses.

The third video was taken some five hours later and showed two men being met by the 'shirts' in the foyer before being joined by the third. The two Caucasian men were shaking the hand of the Arabic looking man before leaving through the entrance.

The CCTV camera then zoomed in on a black leather folder that had been left on a small table near the men's room.

Lamb turned his attention back to the photos and looked at the 'names on the first;
- o   Mr Disney
- o   Mr Drayton Manor
- o   Mr Zawraa

He took a swig of his brandy and studied the remaining photos,

Enlarging the image of the second he could see it was of a document, it was titled;

'The Bikini Project'

The next seven photos were of typewritten documents and he was about to discard number eight, the accidental shot, when something caught his eye. Although the bottom half was blurred as though the subject was too close, he could just discern a reflection on what could be a glass door. He enlarged it and his grip tightened on the phone and a shudder went through him.

He could just make out the white short sleeved shirt and sunglasses of a man standing close to the camera. Part of his right hand was visible and it appeared to be holding something black, possibly a gun. As if to confirm his suspicion he could just make out a finger protruding through what looked like a trigger guard. Checking the photo's 'properties' revealed it had been taken just eleven minutes before the stranger had died!

If ever he needed any proof of the shirts' involvement in the death of the stranger, there it was and with that came the realisation that he was dangerously out of his depth!

He seriously thought about going to the police but he remembered how calmly the shirts had spoken to the police when the man had died, anyway that wouldn't satisfy his thirst for revenge.

Fate's dice hit the board and spun!

***

On the far side of Nerja the shirts were tucking into a meal at Maria Bonita's a little treat to sooth Filip's angry brow.

Edmond Warling looked at his blonde companion gulping down red wine, juice from the skewered chicken running down his chin. 'Must you always eat like a pig Filip we have plenty of time'

Wojtek looked up at the older man opposite and sneered 'Plenty of time you say, well it will take plenty of time for that fool to die' In his mind Warling was soft, a good planner yes, but too soft and he also had a holier than thou attitude, theirs was a partnership of tolerance and convenience. Neither man was respectful of women or men when it came to relationships, in fact both had a leaning towards sexual violence and used either for gratification. One day though Wojtek knew he would kill his companion as payment for all the condescending insults he'd endured, until then however they worked well together.

Edmond Warling sensed the young Croatian staring at him but ignored it. He'd seen that look many times before. He also knew the day would eventually come when they would have to settle accounts with each other and he'd already planned for the event!

Born in the shadow of Windsor Castle, an only child of upper-class parents, it was only natural that Benjamin Markus-Harrington would go to Eton. There, he achieved his degree in Psychological and Behavioural Sciences at Cambridge. His qualifications and IQ of 147 marked him out as being just the type for recruitment to MI5 and he climbed quickly through the ranks in the dark offices of the Millbank 'Citadel'. The salary he received afforded him a small penthouse in Covent Garden, where he was a regular visitor to the Royal Opera House.

This was in direct contrast to the alternate side of his character. That surfaced in the seedy little apartment he also owned in Lambeth under an assumed name. It was the perfect location to satiate his carnal fetishes.

His superiors had initially chosen to ignore the rumours of his sexual predilections, that is, until a neighbour alerted the police to noises that had been coming from the Lambeth premises the previous night. Not getting an answer, the police forced the door and were greeted to a scene of which nightmares are founded. Harrington, wearing a red leather mask, was passed out naked on the floor, surrounded by devices they'd rather not know the use of. Frothy spittle containing flecks of blood, dripped from the corner of his mouth. A second male, also wearing a mask, and naked with the exception of a leather bondage harness, was face up in a cross position, arms and legs bound to special rings fastened to the metal bed posts. From the look of his darkening blue lips and staring red eyes, he had the appearance of someone who was both drugged and dying.

After the paramedics had left with the now stabilized 'victim' and they'd ascertained his true identity, the police passed Harrington on to his employers. The Millbank masters dictated the whole incident to be a regrettable accident, that occurred during abnormal sexual activity. They deemed that responsibility for any punishment 'if needed' lay with them alone … they received no argument from the Met!

From that moment; he was to be known under the alias of Edward Warling aged 53 years. He was also now the property of the secretive 'CLA' department, and was theirs to use as they wished. There would be no records of any past and if checked, even his passport would appear forged

As with all of their field operatives, he had become a 'deniable asset'

***

Lamb studied the names again; he had a niggling at the back of his mind.

- o Mr
  Disney.
- o Mr
  Drayton-
  Manor
- o Mr Zawraa

The words Disney and Dayton-Manor had triggered it, his first thought had been 'Theme parks' 'Disneyland' 'Drayton Manor Park' were obvious, but Zawraa meant nothing to him, so following his initial hunch he googled it.

'Zawraa sc' an Iraqi football team 'Iraq?' faint bells rang in his mind so he scrolled further down and there it was, Zawraa Park Baghdad, 'zoo and theme park' ... bingo!

Lamb let his thoughts come to the fore; theme parks? English, American, Iraqi? Code names? This had to be about more than just roller coasters.

People get thrilled not killed, don't they?

He examined the seven photos of the pages from the folder, by zooming in he could read them clearly enough.

Each was headed The Bikini Project' and in the bottom left hand corner were the numbers 1 of 21, 2 of 21 up to 7 of 21

.

The first page appeared to be an agenda of seven headings;

- o   Overview of Project Bikini
- o   White Sands Deception Strategy
- o   Aqua Slide Global (ASG) Compliance
- o   Aqua Tarin Logistical Analysis
- o   M1003 (MGM-31C) – (SS-1d) Modification Requirements
- o   Sustainability Projections Third Party Funding
- o   Extraction Policy

The second and third pages were titled 'Overview of Project Bikini' and generally described the plan to upgrade an existing Water Park 'Aqua Tarin' as part of the Coalition Redevelopment Strategy. One long section concerned the shipment of Waterslide tubes to Aqua Tarin using Coalition Assets.

Those alarm bells were getting louder!

He suddenly became more alert, the use of the terms 'Coalition' and 'Assets' stood out, it suggested government, more alarmingly it suggested Military!

Lamb put down his mobile phone and walked to the bar and ordered chilli con carne with rice and a large beer. It still didn't make sense to him and so far, he'd found nothing to warrant any killing. However, brandy and an empty stomach certainly wasn't going to make it any clearer.

He looked at the fourth fifth and sixth pages titled 'White Sands Deception Strategy' this mentioned;

- o 'White Sands Lake Leisure Facility, Delaware Ohio'

- o 'White Sands National Park, Southern New Mexico'

The word 'Deception' intrigued Lamb and it soon became apparent that the general plan or 'strategy' was to order some equipment for the former but divert it to the latter. These were innocent sounding locations, so why the deception? And what was the connection between the 'Aqua Tarin Water Park' and a 'US National Park?' the bells were constant now.

Finally, he examined the last image of a page titled 'Aqua Slide Global (ASG) Compliance: It began by stating their business as 'Manufacturers and suppliers of Aqua Parks worldwide' with their head office in Toronto Canada. The text mentioned both their suitability for the project and ability to produce the required equipment. This composed of four fibreglass cylindrical water slides, each section 12metre long, and 1.8metres in diameter. They were to be addressed for delivery to White Sands Lake, Delaware Ohio, and would be shipped by the customer.

Lamb read this page a few times, it seemed odd that any customer, government linked or not, would dictate the exact specification to a company that specialises in this type of equipment. There was no mention of a site visits or supporting structure. Also, it seemed unusual for the customer to collect the equipment themselves … unless they wanted to deliver it to a different location than specified, with no one being any the wiser!

Those alarm bells weren't getting any quieter!

But he still had no idea why someone would kill to conceal this information. All that was about to change!

***

The two shirts had showered and were getting dressed, it was early evening and Wojtek had been champing at the bit, impatient to punish the Englishman who had insulted him.

The older one put his fingers on Wojtek's bare chest 'Relax Filip, first we'll find him, then take him somewhere discreet … just for a discussion you understand' he tapped the side of his nose with his finger and smiled 'Of course you do'

Blue eyes said nothing, he didn't need to, they understood each other implicitly.

Warling continued 'Our friend shouldn't be too hard to trace, after all we know quite a lot about him' he paused for emphasis 'He is English and his first name is Martin, he's mid to late 50's and judging by his accent and sports attire, comes from Liverpool. He also likes a drink but doesn't look the sort to wander too far from the local bars and' ... he stopped and looked across the room.

Wojtek was lifting his travel bag onto the bed,

Tersely, Warling snapped at him 'Filip, I need your full concentration just for one minute!' then continued, impatient to show off 'What is greatly in our favour, is that he was eating sardines for one' he let the significance of this statement sink in 'So in all probability he is a loner... and finally he was sweaty and dishevelled, plus the restaurant owner said he'd had a long day, which could suggest he had only just arrived. If so, possibly from John Lennon airport on a Ryanair flight' again the pause for effect 'Filip with so much information and the resources available to us, it will be very easy to identify and find him. Now let us examine what information he might know about our business. That stupid night manager wouldn't have had time to say too much to him, if anything at all' He paused again considering the options. 'We do however think he has the man's phone, otherwise why follow him down the hill to the cliffs, why abandon his meal?' he nodded towards his young friend 'We can eliminate the bar owner' they both laughed at the irony of what he'd just said 'As whilst we suspected he was hiding something from us, we found no phone in the restaurant'

At this point Wojtek raised his head, he could now contribute 'I saw a phone in the Englishman's hand, it must have been the one we are looking for, I'm sure he had another in his breast pocket, why have two? If the police hadn't arrived so soon, I'd have taken it off him'

'Exactly Filip you did well to spot tha, I'm proud of you'

Wojtek inwardly baulked at yet another condescending remark.

'But what is done is done' he smiled; they were friends again. 'We can't know for certain what is on that phone, but I did interrupt the manager taking pictures of the documents before he ran' again, he was showing off 'And the documents in the folder we recovered were not in the correct order'.

Wojtek reached into his Pineider calfskin travel bag and pulled out two matching soft leather pouches. He handed one to Warling, then opened his own and took out a small black semi-automatic pistol. Next he retrieved four spare magazine clips and a box of loose ammunition. After checking the working parts and confirming a full magazine of six bullets, he chambered a round and clicked the safety on. He then removed the magazine and replaced the chambered round therefore giving him a capacity of seven. Next, he reached behind to clip it inside his jean's waistband at the small of his back. He now had all the tools he needed.

Following the actions of the younger man Warling removed his weapon from its leather pouch and carried out the same procedure. The guns were close combat Taurus Curve .380 semi-automatics and were unique in that they were designed for concealment. Having no sharp angles or protruding edges and with a curved shape, they fitted snuggly to the torso using the attached belt clip. They also had an inbuilt torch and laser.

Whilst both carried guns, they used them sparingly, they were spectres, ghosts, they didn't exist, people they encountered died through accidents … *bullets were forensic and rarely accidental!*

He continued talking 'When we get to the bars, I'll enter each one on my own, and we'll do the same as always; you stay out of sight but in view of the entrance. If he gets past me, just follow him and alert me using the phone tracker, then I'll follow you until we get him isolated'.

Donning Cashmere sweaters and nodding to each other in readiness, they walked out of the apartment and into the night, guided by vicious intent.

***

After dining Lamb felt more civilised. It was dark now and being in the shadows of the bar relaxed him. His view of the carpark was excellent, the lamps were just bright enough to identify any vehicle coming on to it, though not sufficient to expose his own position.

It was time to get more answers 'Aqua Tarin' was an unusual name and mention of the 'Coalition' redevelopment strategy puzzled him … so he googled it;

'Aqua Tarin' the best Water Park in Kurdistan' its website read, and it was situated at a place called Erbil in Iraq. 'Iraq? Coalition? Assets? He'd heard those three words used together before. So, it was a real water park, in a real location, and apparently the right sort of project for redevelopment. So why the secrecy, something like that was a good news story … wasn't it?

Next, he googled 'White Sands Lake Leisure Facility'

***

It was whilst he was concentrating on the phone's screen, that a black X5, its lights switched off, silently coasted onto the carpark and positioned itself between two camper vans. The occupants both wearing matching white shirts under cashmere sweaters nimbly climbed out and using stealth gained through experience, made their way back towards the exit.

White Sands Lake appeared to be just that, a Lake with a large sandy beach. The Aqua Park consisted of a few small inflatable slides and obstacles, but certainly nothing grand enough to warrant the equipment mentioned.

He then googled White Sands National Monument; 'White Sands National Monument, New Mexico, like no place on earth! 275 square miles of white sand desert, the world's largest Gypsum dune field'. His mind froze and he had to re-read the next line several times to ensure he'd got it right;

'Occasionally the road into the monument may close, due to missile testing!'

He hadn't seen that coming. Coalition? Iraq? Missile Testing?

A man entering the bar suddenly caught his eye, a crisp white collar showing above a green sweater and blue designer jeans. He was asking Hannah the chef a question, as she delivered food to a table near the door. She shook her head and pointed to the bar and Alison. He glanced around as he approached the bar, trying to adjust his eyes to the dim lighting.

Lamb's heartbeat increased and his instinct signalled alarm and anger, but his alcohol level calmed him almost immediately. He knew that any sudden movement would almost certainly attract the man's attention, so he waited until he leaned forward to talk to Ali. Then slowly Lamb slipped out of the back door, down the steps and onto the carpark, furious with himself at his failure to spot the X5. He could now see it in the distance and for all he knew the second shirt could be poised in the dark waiting for him. Keeping to the shadows he rounded a corner and paused, watching and listening for anyone approaching. Apart from a girl walking a small dog some way off he could see no one.

Now he urgently needed a hiding place, they could be down here within seconds! Just to the right of where he stood was a large thicket of Bamboo. At 10ft high and 20ft long it was an ideal place to conceal himself. He pushed deep into the plant and ignoring the bugs, crouched down and pulled the stalks across his face and body until he was sure he couldn't be seen. From this position, he watched as both shirts appeared on the carpark frantically searching for him. The lack of local knowledge had caught them unawares, frustrated they turned and headed back towards the bar.

As they climbed the steps the older of the two turned to his friend 'Do not fret Filip it is of no great consequence, I have a plan that will bring him to us'

Lamb caught his breath, as he watched the younger of the two tuck something black into the back of his jeans, it didn't take a genius to work out what it was!

It was now beyond serious; it was deadly and it was scary.

Lamb stayed where he was, afraid to move, insects were crawling over his bare arms and feet, and his mind was in turmoil. But even though he was scared he also wanted revenge on those who had killed his friend!

Ten minutes later he saw the shirts climb into the X5 and drive off.

***

Fourteen hundred miles away, just down the road from the Cenotaph in London, another frightened man was taking a call on his secure phone, his hands were shaking and the colour had drained from his face.

'Pontin you assured me there was no way this could happen! Do you honestly think we'd have agreed to it otherwise! You bloody promised! And now you tell me there's a minor hiccup over some bloody idiot losing a folder?' he took a deep breath 'Minor hiccup? Lost folder? we've been planning this for two years for Christs sake!' he looked heavenwards 'How the hell am I supposed to tell the Americans and the Iraqis that it's all gone wrong because a total dickhead couldn't hold a folder and have a piss at the same time! and anyway how hard would it have been for your people to have checked that nothing was left behind? you said they were the best for the job'

He paused, but when he spoke again the recipient could detect fear in his voice. 'If this gets out you might just as well top yourself do you hear!' The pause at the other end annoyed him even more 'For God's sake are you listening to me?' He gripped the phone even tighter his voice choking in his throat 'Do you not get it? I don't give a damn who lost the folder for all I bloody care it could have been Queen Victoria 'Who' doesn't matter! he rolled his eyes skyward again 'Yes well you make sure it is sorted' a pause 'And Pontin' he spat the next line through gritted teeth 'If you don't, we're both on borrowed time, you do understand that' it was a threat not a question and the man at the other end knew it.

Mr Churchill slammed the phone down on the desk and slumped back into the plush green Chesterfield. 'Oh God' he sighed to himself, anger intermingling with his fear 'Oh my God!'

He was speaking from his secure communications office, an isolated lead and steel lined safe zone, for which there were only three passes to access it. He had one, his close protection officer another, the third was kept in a sealed cabinet in case of national emergency. No conversations could be heard from it nor recorded in it, also his phones were scrambled through a complex system of encryptions that made the enigma device look like connect four.

'Please sort it' he whispered, his fist clenched tightly, the fingernails digging into his palm.

The red mobile phone rang, startling him, it could only be one person. He let it ring a few times to compose himself then picked it up wincing at the pain from his hand 'Good morning Mr Lincoln I was just about to call you'

Fate had found its target and zeroed in on the bullseye!

***

Breaking out from the cover of the bamboo, Lamb brushed himself down before walking back into the Rack and Ruin bar. Warily he scanned the customers, from now on he daren't take any chances.

'Oh, there you are, did you see your friends? only one minute you were here and the next you'd gone, I assumed you'd taken them onto the car park' it was Ali from the bar 'Bye the way, has the younger one always been a bit odd? I mean sorry if they're close mates, but ugh, he gave me the creeps … those eyes!'

Lamb smiled at her 'It's ok they're certainly not friends, it's quite complicated, but I saw the older one talking to you, mind if I ask what he said?'

'Not at all, he described you quite accurately really, said you were friends and wanted to surprise you, I thought it was odd when he went out into the street to call the other one in, sorry did I do wrong telling them you were here?'

Lamb allowed himself a smile 'No not your fault, but if they come in again could you tell them you've not seen me since, please. One day I'll explain but I'm not sure of anything myself yet'

She studied him intently 'You really are worried aren't you, look has this got anything to do with Sergio the owner of Quixote's only you asked about him earlier'

'Maybe, but please don't ask any more questions, the less you know at this stage the better for everyone, sorry'

Ali nodded and went back to help Bibi cleaning the glasses, curious but aware that pushing it wouldn't get any more answers. Little did she know that something she'd later read in a newspaper; would destroy any trust she'd had in him.

***

Lamb still wanted answers and he was sure they lay in the memory card, however now he couldn't trust himself to spot the shirts if they returned. He needed a secure hiding place to carry on with his

53

research, one with Wi-Fi. Plus, he wasn't going to return to his apartment as he now deemed it too dangerous, so he also had to find somewhere to spend the night.

He'd noticed that by climbing over the adjoining small wall, he could access the outdoor patio of the Los Trillizos Spanish restaurant next door. As they only opened at lunch times he wouldn't be disturbed, plus he could still access R and R's Wi-Fi.

Lamb approached the bar and ordered an opened bottle of red Rioja to take away 'It was late and he didn't have a corkscrew' he also ordered another brandy 'One for the road' Returning to the dark corner of the bar he reflected on his position.

In his pockets, he had 470 euros in notes plus some shrapnel, as well as his bank card and passport. That would sort travelling, plus any food and equipment he might need. He'd have to change his phone, and acquire some 'pay as you go' sim cards for communication, satnav and news, but all told he was in pretty good shape.

He sipped his brandy; it was getting towards closing time and customers were slowly drifting out of the bar. When the girls went outside to collect glasses, he grabbed a steak knife from a yet un-cleared table, and piled the plates up to disguise its loss. Then gripping the wine, he slipped unseen over the wall and sat down so that he was out of sight. Switching on his Blackberry, he dimmed the screen to hide the glow, then looked at the photos again.

Although there were no photographed documents relating to 'M1003 (MGM-31C) - (SS-1d) Modification Requirements' he decided to google it anyway.

The results for M1003 produced various results: from, the carrying of dangerous goods or hazardous waste, to US certification for selling second-hand electronic equipment. He decided to keep an open mind for the time being. Then almost as an after-thought he entered MGM-31C and tapped the search button.

'MGM-31 Pershing II Missile'

The bells had given way to thunder!

A quick summary revealed Pershing Ⅱ to be an Intercontinental Ballistic Missile, Range of 1,100 miles (1,770km) Length 34feet, Diameter 40inches and further down the page, the clincher:

It was launched from the M1003 mobile platform.

He read on, supposedly, all Perishing Missiles had been destroyed as part of the Intermediate-Range Nuclear Forces Treaty of May 1988. It also stated that West Germany also had the missiles, and these were allegedly shipped back to the US for destruction as part of the same agreement.

With mounting tension, he googled SS-1d; the first subject described, was a high strength plastic security strap for some obscure electrical connector. Further down though he saw more damning information;

'SS-1d, Scud C' a Russian vehicle launched short range ballistic missile!

And then the enormity of what he had discovered punched him deep in the pit of his stomach, it was an idea so shocking that he immediately realised why he'd been given a death sentence!

Fate threw a double six!

Bikini! They must have laughed so hard when they chose that name! The irony finally hit him!

'Bikini' skimpy swimwear of the sort you might find in an Aqua Park, designed by a Parisian engineer and named after 'Bikini Atoll'

'Bikini Atoll' one of the Marshall Islands in the Pacific; previously the site of US nuclear weapon testing back in the 40's and 50's

He took a long swallow of his wine. This couldn't be true surely? A numbness had now come over him, this should be the stuff of fiction! However, it was all coming together with a terrible clarity, it even made sense of the killings:

- o Firstly, Georgio the night manager, was murdered after they caught him photographing the documents.

o   Secondly, they couldn't risk letting Sergio live, once he'd had access to the man's mobile in case he understood its contents.

Lamb now had the deadly evidence that could bring down governments and start wars! He realised that even if he gave the phone back or destroyed it they would still kill him for what he 'may' have discovered. By now they must know who he is, after all they had access to border controls, bank accounts and even his own phone! There must be at least two governments wanting him, a 58-year-old widower, dead!

And whilst it scared him, it also pissed him off!

Well he wasn't going to just sit there and wait! No, he had nothing to lose, his life had virtually ended the day Mary died anyway. The establishment had done nothing, no prosecution, no justice, and now they'd also killed the one remaining person he'd called his friend.

At that moment, on a secluded patio in Nerja Spain, Lamb swore an oath of vengeance upon the people at the very top,

Even if he died, they would taste the devil's breath!

He took another big swig of wine wishing it were brandy and listened as the girls locked up the bar for the night. It was safer to stay where he was for a few hours and try to get some sleep, then maybe in the early hours he'd make his way out of Nerja. Before sleep however, he needed a plan. This is where his security experience kicked in. He knew all about deception trails, it was how he'd earned his bread and butter, tracking teams of criminals.

Almost certainly, they'd be watching his bank account, and he was satisfied they wouldn't block it whilst they tracked him, why close a trail needlessly? He decided to make as many withdrawals in as shorter time as possible and at as many ATM's as he could find, whilst leading them in a direction of his choosing. He now switched off his phone and removed the battery, he could use it to his advantage later on, but only once! It would still need ditching, but not before he'd made four more copies of the SD card.

Grabbing some seat cushions from the nearby chairs, he placed them on the floor as a makeshift bed. Then after taking a final swallow of wine, he set the alarm and dropped off to a reluctant sleep.

***

Day 3 … Thursday 28th April 2016

Keep on Running!

Dawn was just breaking when Lamb awoke at 6am. His tongue felt twice its normal size and tasted of sewage. His eyes were full of grit and every bone in his body screamed in torment when he breathed. Not a good start to a war! In the absence of any other liquid he tilted the wine bottle and downed the last few stale dregs, it made him gag but anything to get rid of the sewage. Not far away, at the junction of Calle Pintada and Calle Angustias there was a drinking fountain and he was certain he'd find an empty water bottle or two in the waste bins on the way. These would see him ok, whilst he walked the seven kilometres down the coastline to Torrox Costa. There he'd get breakfast and top up with the few supplies he might need, before going to the cash machine.

He took off his football shirt, ripped the sleeves off and turned it inside out, they may have given the police his description, so he wanted to at least change his appearance even slightly, in case he encountered the Guardia civil or police at this early hour.

After lowering himself down from the wall and walking through the passage to the street he found the binned water bottles as expected and made his way stiffly to the fountain for water. He then crossed the top of Plaza Espana before heading down towards Torrecilla Beach via the Hotel Rue Monica, he was looking for something but it wasn't there. Next, he crossed the dried river bed of the Rio Chillar and followed the beach past the dusty boat yards, the metallic clatter of loose rigging adding melody to rhythm of gentle waves.

It was as he passed the Hotel Marinas on his right and just prior to climbing the steep steps up to the main road, he saw what he'd been seeking. His logic had told him that the shirts would have altered their accommodation arrangements, once their original mission in Nerja had imploded, and they didn't seem the type to stay in any old hostal. It was doubtful they'd stay at the Balcon Hotel; it was too central and would have made them feel very conspicuous among the tourists. The Parador was also out of the equation as they'd killed its manager. There were others but none that would suit their purpose quite like this one; it was very smart, but out of town and with easy access to main roads going in any direction.

He'd now found what he was looking for; a black dusty X5 sitting among forty other vehicles in the hotel carpark!

Lamb checked the area for CCTV cameras, there were two, one at the exit and one on the foyer entrance to monitor taxis collecting or dropping off guests, none were scanning the vehicles. Keeping to the shadows, he made his way warily through the surrounding bushes to the object of his anger. Then crouching low, he punctured each tyre with the steak knife, the sound of escaping air seemingly deafening in his isolation. As a final gesture of defiance, he scratched the letters YNWA on the driver's door, certain they'd understand the message. He wanted them to feel hunted not hunters, that way he hoped at least one of them would start to act irrationally!

Departing back through the bushes, he climbed the steps up to the main road and for the first time since he'd arrived in Spain, he felt satisfaction. The last shroud of darkness was giving way to dawn as he paced himself along the craggy shoreline towards breakfast.

***

Filip Wojtek was irritable, not surprising following the previous evening's activity. Warling had been on his phone for half an hour now. It had been the same over dinner last night, when they'd been told of the Englishman's details:

'Martin Lamb aged 58, widower, born in Liverpool England, arrived on Ryanair flight FR9862 two days ago. Ex- British army; REME (Royal Electrical and Mechanical Engineers) followed by a period overseas, working for a satellite company of the Department of Overseas Development, MTS (Iran) Ltd. There he'd been a Technical Advisor to the Iranian army. Then various other jobs but nothing of real note thought Wojtek. Had a UK sim in his mobile phone with four months left on an EE contract and banked with Lloyds, has done so for 32 years, no Credit cards just Debit'

However, it was the last use of his Visa card that interested them, he'd booked one month's stay at a first-floor apartment on Calle Los Huertos starting date; Tuesday 26th April.

Before going to bed they'd visited the apartment and even rang the buzzer but it was obvious that no one was in. Afterwards they'd parked the car on an adjacent street and taken it turns to keep watch on the front door. As expected, Lamb didn't show! … *the wolves would go hungry tonight!*

Sensing his partner's impatience Warling turned to him 'There is plenty of time Filip we'll have help finding him now, it's just a matter of time, we only have to wait, come I'll explain over breakfast' puzzled Wojtek followed.

They seated themselves as far away from the other guests as possible and between muesli, boiled eggs and fruit, Warling smugly revealed the latest plan.

'I was on the phone a long time yesterday and today, for a very special reason Filip, Mr Pontin our controller and I, have been urgently developing a plan' he looked up at the ceiling 'Not an easy task considering his mood I can tell you. Using our resources back home we have fed some, shall we say, unflattering information about our Mr Lamb to various news outlets across Spain' he let this sink in 'If we've managed to beat the deadlines, that information should appear in the ex-pat newspapers this morning' he cracked the shell of his boiled egg and continued 'We, that is Mr Pontin and I, have agreed that if Lamb was going to use the information we want, two things have so far prevented it'. He took a sip of his strong black coffee and pulled a face at the grainy taste 'Firstly he seems to have some modicum of intelligence, so we believe therefore that he will be reluctant to pass it on without considering very carefully where and how. We believe he won't want to cause unnecessary harm to people' he paused, as a waiter cleared some of the plates off their table 'Secondly, he knows that once he has passed this information on, he'll become an even bigger target from other countries' he let Wojtek absorb his meaning. 'So Filip although time is of the essence, we do still have some' he drank the remainder of his pineapple juice 'Eventually someone will recognize him and call the contact number we have supplied with the article, so his whereabouts will soon be ours. Until then, let us relax and enjoy our stay' seeing his friend's agitation he continued, enjoying the torment 'I shall not tell you what the story in the newspapers will say as it will be a nice surprise for you, but trust me you will love it, anyway my pet, do me a favour and fetch me some more pineapple juice there's a good boy'

***

Considering he once thought fresh air and plain water to be toxic, Lamb had made good time on his walk along the unspoilt craggy shoreline to Torrox, in fact he'd almost enjoyed it. He needn't have worried about the police being curious, there were quite a few joggers and power walkers taking advantage of the cool morning temperatures. His first priority was an English breakfast at the Bus Station Café, with two cups of strong sweet Americano coffee and a fresh orange juice to finish.

Feeling suitably nourished, he went into the toilets to splash water on his face. Then it was over to the cheap 'sell everything' Chinese shop for a small backpack. Added to this he chose four shirts, a pack of underwear, two different colour pairs of lightweight trousers that unzipped below the knees, to turn them into shorts and a floppy hat that could be folded to look like a cap. To finish his clothing choice, he also selected a lightweight weatherproof jacket with large pockets. Joining this collection was a bar of soap some cheap safety razors, a metal nail file and a small bottle of sun cream. Going past the electrical section he added a small roll of electrical insulating tape and in stationary grabbed a small pencil sharpener, finally at the till he asked for two 2GB memory cards.

Further down the road, on the opposite side, he'd spotted a second-hand phone shop. There he bought two cheap mobiles and four 'pay as you go' Movistar sim cards, each loaded with 20 euros. The shop owner unsure as to whether he'd just set up a drug dealer, was never the less happy with his sale, so took the money eagerly.

Better equipped but feeling decidedly sweaty, Lamb made his way down to the beach for a topless dip in the sea followed by a rinse off under the beach shower. Finally, he walked over to a sea front tapas bar and after ordering a large beer used the toilets to get changed. Feeling what he considered to be normal, after gulping down the beer, he ordered another and took in the view.

He examined his purchases, then using the tip of the nail file unscrewed the blade of the pencil sharpener and wound tape around the square end to make a small handle. Next, he folded paper around the sharp end before again wrapping tape around it, this gave him a tiny sheathed knife ideal for concealing in clothing. It was a trick he'd learned off shoplifters who used the blades to cut security tags off clothing. With the blade, he made two tiny slits; one either side of his trousers' elastic waistband.

Using his Blackberry and one of the cheap phones he blue-toothed two more copies of the original SD card and inserted one plus the original and the tiny blade into the slit in the left-hand side of his waist band. The remaining card he inserted into the right-hand slit.

Suddenly, he swore at his own stupidity! Why hadn't it occurred to him? A mistake like this could cost him his life! What would be the first port of call for anyone looking for him? The bus stations or taxi ranks obviously, and he'd just been the only customer in the nearest café. He took a slug of his beer, paid the bill and made his way to the cash machine, a new urgency spurring him on. Waiting until he could see the green and white Alsa bus to Malaga approaching, he withdrew the maximum euros, then hung back until the last of the queue had boarded.

Thankful for the air conditioning, Lamb settled back into his seat confident no one was watching him. The bus was only half full and he'd picked a seat across from the centre exit. Once in the city his first priority was to find a cheap hostal for a couple of nights.

At the third stop an English couple got on and sat in the seat opposite. The man then opened a copy of the 'Sur in English' a free newspaper targeted at the ex-pat community and tourists staying along the Costas. Although Lamb couldn't read the small print, he could see at the bottom of the front page an article that shook him. He clenched his fists and resisted the urge to snatch the paper from the man. He swore under his breath and a tenseness came over him, then slowly it gave way to anger! There was no mistaking it, the picture he was looking at was the same one as in his passport, but it was the caption above it that really enraged him!

'Fugitive Martin Lamb 'Wanted, on suspicion of fraud against vulnerable pensioners!'

This was a new measure of the desperation and ruthlessness of the people pursuing him, rather than deflate him, it had the opposite effect. His first instinct was to turn around, go back, and confront the shirts! Against his better judgement he glanced at the other passengers to see if anyone was looking at him. No one seemed to be taking an interest so he reached into his bag to take out the hat he'd bought.

His original decision was to get off at Malaga bus station, but now he'd get off at the port, which was busier and gave him more options to make his way through the shopping streets and into the bustling heart of the city. He knew from experience that most people in large crowded areas walked almost zombie like, never looking directly at the faces of the people around them. Their only priority was to get to their destination quickly and with the least possible fuss, anyone looking out for him would stand out. Again, his previous experience at spotting criminals would now prove useful.

His initial shock had now receded and he thought about his image in the newspaper. They'd obviously got it from his records, which gave an indication into how far their tentacles reached, and how high up the WMD scandal went. Fortunately for him the photo was seven years old and since then he'd grown a moustache and beard, however anyone studying it very closely would certainly recognize him.

***

Mr Churchill's day wasn't going well;

'**Of** course, Mr Lincoln, there will be an update just as soon as I have one. The truth is I haven't really seen the need, I mean I'm sure it's just a minor irritation, I have our best operatives on it at this very moment' He winced at the tone of the reply 'Well I'm surprised by your action Mr Lincoln, it wasn't necessary to send your men, ours are very capable' again he sensed the tension in the other man's voice 'Yes, obviously we're in this together, and yes I know the chaos this could cause but we all looked into this very closely and considered it a risk worth taking' the voice at the other end was louder now. 'No, I'm not underestimating the seriousness of the situation I am merely refusing to let a minor glitch affect our plans, as I said it will soon be sorted' he paused 'Yes Mr Lincoln and good day to you'

He rose from the chesterfield, perspiration soaking his armpits and walked shakily to the window to stare out at the greyness of a wet London day, the clattering of rain on the windowpane drumming his despair even deeper.

Fate was drumming up a thunderstorm!

***

Filip Wojtek was bored, inaction didn't suit him. Warling could lounge about indefinitely,which was just another of his irritating traits 'I'll take the BMW to the filling station and get it washed and fuelled, in case we have to move suddenly'

Warling smiled, he knew how his companion disliked inactivity 'Good idea Filip, and could you pick up a copy of the 'Sur in English' you know the free paper, hopefully the surprise I promised you will be in it'

The first thing Wojtek noticed were the deflated tyres, then as his anger mounted, he saw the six-inch-high letters scratched into the driver's door, then all hell hit the fan.

Bursting with rage he made his way back through the foyer and into the hotel lounge, where

Warling was selecting a book to read. 'I am going to kill the Englishman slowly, in fact very slowly!' he hissed 'You will not stop me Edmond I will kill him; I will not be depraved!'

Warling smiled at his companion's grammatical error, but the use of his Christian name alerted him to the depth of Filip's anger, although he couldn't at that stage imagine what could have triggered it.

'Calm down Filip and tell me what has made you so angry'

Red faced and furious, Wojtek described what he'd found, angry spittle spraying from his lips. 'YNWA what is that, what does it mean, it can only be the Englishman, he is haunting us yes?

Warling shook his head, Filip always mixed his words when angry 'The letters mean 'You'll Never Walk Alone' a Liverpool football slogan and yes, the Englishman is indeed taunting us. You shall have your opportunity Filip, that I promise. In the meantime, I was fortunate enough to find a copy of the English newspaper on a coffee table. If you were to now read it, I'm certain it may lighten your mood somewhat'

The opportunity he mentioned would present itself sooner than they realized!

***

The officer at passport control in Malaga airport eyed the two Americans warily, each of their passports described them as Lawyers but something wasn't right. For a start they were both mid 40's and heavily tanned and the bodies beneath their neatly pressed t-shirts were honed from many hours in the gym. In fact, they reminded him of soldiers or policemen, rather than someone who spent their days in offices or courtrooms. But it was their hands that gave them away. As each one handed over his passport, he'd noticed that on both of them, the web of skin between the thumb and forefinger on the right hand was rougher and darker than normal. It was something he recognized very well, having spent many hours firing his semi-automatic handgun on the pistol range. It could only have been caused by the recoil mechanism coming back, as the gun ejected one shell and loaded another, whilst at the same time depositing tiny amounts of powder residue and oil on the skin.

Lynden Harkant and Jaycee Cropfeld were old school. The only rules were their rules and nothing or anyone else mattered. Finesse wasn't in their dictionary, violence and death was. The only instruction they'd received was 'get whatever information he has, then neutralise the problem!'

SCOPE (Specialist Counter Operations Priority Events) had given them the latest intelligence information on the target: His name, description, the area he was believed to be in and that he was to be dealt with as quickly as possible. As with the British operators, they'd been privy to just basic details as to why they were hunting their prey. Their missions were run on a 'need to know' basis and it suited them that way. They also knew of the newspaper article accusing Lamb of being a fraudster, but that was a negative in their eyes, it made him too public. What they couldn't understand was the difficulty the two Brits were having; it was just one annoying Limey tourist for Christ's sake!

Their weapons had already arrived in a diplomatic bag. Harkant's a Sig Sauer P229 Legion with SD9 suppressor and Cropfeld's a Wilson Combat Sentinel and Rimfire silencer. Both 9mm semi-automatic compact weapons, designed with concealment in mind, but powerful enough to fulfil their assignment should it get messy.

However, the main weapon in their arsenal was the Gulfstream 1V executive jet (tail number N85FM) waiting at Getafe Air Base, a NATO military airfield just outside of Madrid. It was fuelled and ready to take Lamb on a rendition flight to a country of their choosing, his immediate death was the lesser option!

In the taxi feeling rough and tired from the effects of the long flight, Harkant took a Modafinil tablet and passed one to his companion. It was going to be a long day so they'd collect their car from the consulate motor pool sometime tomorrow.

During the next hour, three phone calls were received, one by Harkant and another by Warling, two men forty miles apart.

The third call was answered by a man heading a top-secret department whose offices were in Great Peter Street, Millbank, London, almost 1500 miles away from them both.

***

Having obtained a copy of 'Sur in English' from the brochure board outside the tourist information office on Plaza de la Marina, Lamb made his way to the Antiqua Casa de Guardia, the oldest bar in Malaga, for a glass of wine and a chance to read the full article about himself. His name was just below the photograph and the storyline stated that he was suspected of targeting pensioners in order to steal their life savings. It said he was wanted for questioning by the Serious Overseas Fraud Office (SOFO) in the UK. It also emphasized the importance of not approaching him but to immediately contact the 'special phone number' given at the end of the article.

Feeling calmer after the alcohol, he studied article for a while. Considering that he knew the details in it to be false, he also surmised there was a good chance that the 'special' number for the so called

'Serious Overseas Fraud Office' a department he'd never heard of, would be too.

With anger dictating his actions, he decided to call it and test its authenticity.

In the oak panelled office on Milbank, headquarters of the vaguely named 'Core Logistical Analytics (CLA), a confident male voice answered. For a split second it faded then returned, as though he'd turned away from the phone's speaker. Signalling to someone else in the room maybe?

'Hello Serious Overseas Fraud Office Pontin speaking, may I have your name please?'

Lamb resisted the urge to launch profanities at him 'You know my name already and you need to listen, not talk' he took a deep breath 'I also know this is being tracked, so don't bother …'
The voice cut him off 'I'm sorry but unless you give me your name we can't continue' this time, it was said with authority.

Lamb gripped his phone tighter 'Ok, if that's how you want to play it, you have a think about Project Bikini and I'll call back in two hours' He switched the phone off, then crossed the river towards the Maria Zambrano shopping centre and the railway station within it…. Beneath that, the Renfe line to Fuengirola.

Some thirty minutes, later he phoned the number again. The same voice answered, but this time his tone had changed 'You said two hours I haven't had a chance to…'

Lamb interrupted 'Contact the heavies' here in Spain and tell them to back off or Bikini becomes front page news in the Jerusalem Star!

'I don't have any idea wha …'

Lamb cut across him again 'Look Pontin I don't know what your connection is to this but …' he stopped suddenly 'Whoa … let me rewind a second, you're no common or garden office boy are you! Whatever the information is that you think I have, it's so secret that you're killing people for it … so no way would a minion be privy to this! Plus, you're using a similar alias to the three wise men at the hotel' he laughed 'No mate, you're in this up to your neck, aren't you? I reckon the clowns here are yours, this is your circus and you are the ring master!' He rang off again and walked through the barriers towards the platform escalators.

Twenty-five minutes later, he was downing a large beer in the Viking bar at Torremolinos and making his third phone call to Pontin.

Without waiting for the voice at the other end to answer, he gritted his teeth and spoke quietly 'Listen in, I know you're still tracking this call and I know you'll have contacted your pets over here, so I won't say too much' again he fought the urge to launch a tirade of abuse at the man who had probably ordered the killing of his friend

'I have what you want, I know what it means and I know how to use it, and you're pissing me right off with your crap ok!'

Pontin spoke calmly 'I have no idea what this so-called project Bikini is Mr Lamb, or may I call you Martin. Yes of course I know your name, oh and by the way I was so sorry to hear of your loss, naturally by that I mean your wife' he was tormenting him, demonstrating his power. 'We wish merely to talk to you about a mobile phone and some information you may have inadvertently received, nothing more than that' he paused for a second to let it sink in and buy time 'We don't see that you have done anything wrong Martin, so why don't you just meet with my men and discuss this face to face. You can even choose the venue if you like, it is not a problem' a slight pause again 'Yet' he waited for the last word to register 'We can then resolve the other issue, namely your notoriety in the tabloids at the same time'

Lamb fought down the urge to shout, Pontin had just confirmed his status and ability to obtain personal information about him.
He spoke slowly, accentuating every word. 'Listen Pontin whoever or whatever you are, firstly you know by now that I've seen what's on the phone. I somehow think it's a little bit late for discussions with those

poncey slaves of yours … who by the way are toting guns. Also, you killed my friend and for that, you will all pay the price. It will not alter whatever happens' He paused to let that sink in 'Thirdly you need to tell *your boss* and we both know who that is' he'd emphasized the last few words to drive them home 'That I know what the Bikini Project is. I also know that there are missiles involved and I know that the destination is in Iraq. You can deny it all you like, but I can think of a few countries that would be very interested in just part of what I have. So, for a start, you kill that story in the papers by saying it was a mistaken identity … after that who knows'

Pontin jumped in, afraid to lose the opportunity to reason with him 'Of course I will, it was a clumsy error of judgement on our part but I still have no idea wha…'

'Keep this line open you'll need it, time's running out!'

Lamb ended the call, switched his phone to flight mode and walked back to the station to catch the Renfe back to Malaga.

Once there, he walked along the main road away from the train station towards the port area and the bus stops there. He didn't want to risk using the main bus station in case they had it under surveillance. At the kiosk he used his debit card to pay the full fare to Granada, knowing already that it would be stopping at various towns on route, including Nerja. The third bus to arrive had the destinations of Motril and Granada displayed, so he climbed aboard and took a seat near to the centre exit door, welcoming the coolness of the air conditioning.

Some 26 kilometres away from Malaga and 10 kilometres before its next stop he switched on the Blackberry, removed the sd card, cleared all messages and images and took it off flight mode. Then he wedged it deep down into the gap between the seat and side panel, where it wouldn't be easily found. Arriving at Torre de Mar some twelve minutes later, he joined a crowd of tourists and disembarked through the centre door, then watched, as both bus and mobile disappeared for the long journey inland.

Twenty minutes after that, he'd found a small hostal and checked in. Later, having freshened up he made his way to Bar Viva International a small place tucked into the corner of an apartment building, for much needed beers and Brandy. Sitting in the darkest corner he took out his copy of 'Sur in English' and using it as a diversion started to read through it.

It was on the third page, that he saw the story he'd never wanted to read, At the same time as dreading it's content, he was drawn into it like some macabre hypnosis;

'Nerja Bar Owner dies in Tragic Accident'

It then went on to describe how Sergio Manos the bar owner, was killed, after coming into contact with a live wire on a faulty light switch, whilst mopping the wet floor. It also stated that investigators had found two more such switches in the premises, suggesting neglect. Further down the column, it briefly noted that it was the second death of a local man in 24 hours but the incidents were not believed to be related. For a while he just stared out into the street. Visions of his friend's last moments invaded the memory of their last conversation, and slowly his raw fury returned.

He continued to read the newspaper, hoping the barmaid hadn't noticed his anguish and sweats, when a second article caught his eye. He re-read it several times, trying to free the faint alert, that was trying to rise above the confusing mush of data, in the depths of his brain.

Slowly the thought surfaced and a plan formed in his mind.

Initially it seemed crazy, but the more he thought about it the less ridiculous it seemed. Anyway, it was better than no plan at all, however in order to act upon it he needed to buy time.

Before going to bed, he rang his Blackberry from one of his spare phones and set a chain of events in motion that he hoped would buy him those vital hours he needed.

***

Two operators thousands of miles apart, saw the onscreen alert they'd been waiting for and summoned their respective supervisors. Both the Pentagon and GCHQ now thought Lamb was on the move!

The Pentagon were the quickest to react and a call was made to Lynden Harkant.

'Yep got that, he's on his way back to Nerja, you sure? no problem we'll get on route straight away, just inform us once you've got his exact location or any other developments' he turned to his compatriot 'C'mon Jaycee we got us a Lamb to roast' both men smiled, at ease with the mission.

Lynden Harkant though was puzzled, after spending an hour picking up their car and driving towards Nerja 'SCOPE Central' had informed him, that the person they were seeking had only stopped there for a few minutes. He now appeared to be heading along the A7 motorway towards Granada. Judging by the various stops he'd made they were guessing he was on public transport; it suggested a bus.

'Why would he risk going back through Nerja Jaycee? And why all of a sudden turn on his mobile? This guy is either very stupid or we're being played' he took in a final view of the receding coastline knowing that shortly it would be replaced by the snow-capped Sierra Nevada mountain range.

Jaycee made no comment, but just shrugged, he was concentrating on getting to Granada before the bus.

Harkant dialled a number and when it was answered spoke firmly 'Look I know we prefer to act independently but as this is code 5, maybe we should contact the limeys here on the ground' he paused nodding 'Yep I totally agree I mean they must be sharing intel higher up or how would we have all his details? We don't have to tell them everything we do, but on the other hand we don't want them fouling up the operation do we!' he listened to the response 'Ok sure, after you've spoken with them get back to me'

***

Edward Warling absorbed the information he'd just received from his superior Mr Pontin: GCHQ had reported that Lamb had used his debit card to buy a bus ticket to Granada and his phone had also been activated. The direction of travel suggested he was heading back towards Nerja. This knowledge held little comfort to him and Filip, who were already showing Lamb's photo in the many bars and restaurants of Torremolinos, following Lamb's earlier call to Pontin. Now they had to retrace their steps and track a bus going to Granada via Torre de Mar, Nerja and Motril.

Another call came in from Pontin; it had been decided that they were to link up with the Americans 'No it wasn't open to debate, this was of the highest priority, he was sending contact numbers'

It just wasn't Warling's day ... the bloody Yanks didn't even speak the same English!

***

Day 4 … Friday 29ᵗʰ April 2016

To Catch a Thief!

Lamb awoke early, tired from the recurring nightmare. In it he saw flames in the shape of a man, its mouth a distorted black oval, the eyes two white hot circles, wide with terror. It was beckoning to him, pleading to know the reason for its journey to hell, and the voice he heard was Sergio's.

Lamb knew this would now be with him for the rest of his life. It would cut across what remaining memories he had of Mary and for that he cursed them.

There could be no going back now!

Ironically, whilst destroying the few remaining things he had sought to live for, his enemies had given him an even bigger cause to survive … revenge!

On top of that they had taken away his fear and replaced it with a deadly cunning born of hatred.

It pleased him that they thought he was running and he wanted it that way. At some point he would not only stop but turn against them and dish out retribution.

In the future he would want his adversaries to find him, but it would be at a time and place of his choosing. He would summon them to their fate and he wouldn't stop until he reached the very top of those responsible. If governments were to crumble so be it, but no more innocent people must die.

First though he needed help and currently there was only one person he could think of.

Washing but not shaving, he dressed in fresh clothes, put on his floppy hat and Ray-Bans and checked himself over. He was satisfied that he now looked like every other traveller to the Costas. Opening the newspaper, that he'd taken from the bar the day before, he again read the article that had caught his eye. And then tore out the photograph of the man it referred to.

Feeling a little more confident, he set out into the cool morning air to find the necessary means to achieve his aim.

Ignoring breakfast, Lamb made his way to the taxi rank opposite the bus station and asked to be taken to the Plaza de la Marina opposite Malaga port. On arriving, he crossed over to the ticket office and purchased a ticket to Fuengirola. Some twelve minutes later, he was settled down in the air-conditioned comfort of the Socibus luxury coach. He would use the 50-minute journey to concentrate on his plan, he needed to get the details exactly right if he was to pull it off. If he didn't, then god knows what would happen, but one thing was certain the time for running had gone.

For the second part of his journey, he caught the number 60 bus from Fuengirola to Marbella and a taxi from there to Puerta Banus. He figured he'd need at least a week to set the first part of his plan in motion. The previous night, using' booking.com' he'd managed to secure a relativity cheap deal, for six nights at the Hotel Dona Catalina, which was within easy walking distance to the port.

After checking in and paying cash in advance for the six nights, he reassured himself that he hadn't been recognised and did a quick scan of his room. Satisfied, he then set out towards the harbour area to do a bit of essential shopping. He returned one hour later, to get showered and neatly trim his beard. Then having splashed on a small amount of Cartier aftershave, he changed into his newly purchased 'Ralph Lauren' pale blue casual shirt and cream 'Chinos' before putting on a pair of white 'Boss' loafers. As a finishing touch, he tied a dark blue sweater over his shoulders and put on a reasonably priced Panama hat. Finally, he checked himself in the mirror and was quite pleased with the 'smart casual' result.

Whilst he would blend in nicely with the 'motor launch' crowd on the harbour front, he didn't want to stand out as part of the mega rich 'Yachting set'.

Before going out again, he carried out the usual routine of opening small slits in both sides of the waist grip of the Chinos into which he placed his sd cards and tiny blade. Then into his pockets, he put the saved newspaper article, along with his passport, money and one of the cheap mobile phones he'd bought in Torrox, now loaded with a new Movistar pay as you go sim card. He'd also purchased some blank business cards from Boutique Montblanc and on twenty-five of them had written his last name, phone number and the simple cryptic message 'I can help you' these he also pocketed.

Thus, attired and equipped, he made his way to the marina and the Don Leonne restaurant, where he'd booked a table on the journey down. It was the sort of place where he imagined his intended target would dine. Anyway, he had to start somewhere. He ordered the Sole in Champagne sauce and a glass of Rueda: It wasn't his usual tipple but he'd browsed the menu on-line and chosen what he perceived to be an average choice for the establishment. From his table he could see both the entrance and the promenade around the harbour. This was important if events unfolded as he expected them to. When the waitress brought him his meal, he showed her the picture from the newspaper, and asked if the man featured had ever visited the restaurant. He explained that it was an old friend of his from the army days whom he wanted to surprise. She was unsure but agreed to take it into the kitchen to see if any of the other staff recognised him. The result was negative, so after his meal, he booked the same table for the remainder of the week then left to visit other bars in the vicinity of the marina. At each location he asked the staff the same question, and although he got a zero response, he always left a card. He repeated the same routine each evening, always starting at Don Leonne's before heading out to different bars. Each time he would fan out further from the marina before retiring back to the hotel around midnight.

He knew he was taking a risk; that the shirts would eventually find him but he was always cautious and constantly tuned in to his surroundings. He'd subconsciously scan his immediate area for 'flight or fight' options and select secure locations to reach in the event of trouble. This way he wouldn't lose valuable seconds of indecision when danger arrived.

***

The atmosphere around the table was strained to say the least, as Warling, Wojtek, Harkant and Cropfeld studied each other. Neither wanting to start the conversation. It had been a difficult couple of days for them all, chasing shadows to Granada and back, along the bus route.

Eventually, Warling broke the silence 'Gentlemen we all know this is not how we wanted to work, but those higher up than us, have decided, in their wisdom, that we must' He paused to make sure he had everyone's attention 'Therefore we need a strategy that makes best use of our resources, both here in Spain and back in our respective homelands'

Harkant nodded 'Ok I agree, so let's share what we know up to now, then we can each spell out our end games'

Thus, having ascertained who the dominant figure was in each pairing, they proceeded to make plans for the future of Martin Lamb.

All parties agreed that prior to disposing of him, an interrogation would be both preferable and beneficial!

They also agreed;
- o That like themselves, their respective headquarters had concluded, there was a high probability that Lamb was still in Spain and somewhere on the Costa del Sol.
- o That he was somewhere along the Renfe line from Malaga to Fuengerola, and this was based on the following information;
- o Each of his communications had been from sites in close proximity to stations on that route.
- o A check on his joint bank account and debit cards showed that with the exception

of two visits to Greece in 2003/4 Lamb and his wife had always come to this region of Spain.

It was decided that one team would go to the end of the line at Fuengerola and start from there, whilst the others would begin at the Malaga end and investigate each location down the line.

***

Fidgeting with his solid gold Tibaldi fountain pen, a present from some Saudi Sheik in gratitude for a favour he could no longer recall. Mr Churchill waited impatiently for the dreaded phone call from his American counterpart.

Although expected, it still startled him when it came!

'Mr Lincoln how are you today? I see congress is still messing you about over your latest fina …' the voice at the other end cut him off 'Of course I understand, but this was hardly my fault. Might I remind you that there were three men at that meeting, one of whom was yours and it was the Iraqi who left the folder!' he was cut off again 'Yes they are working together and because of that I foresee a rapid conclusion to this unfortunate episode' he listened to the curt reply 'Ok, let us then at least agree; that when and not if! Lamb is caught' he will be fully debriefed by both our sides' he froze for a second 'Of course we both understand the alternative; however, I don't think we should speak of it yet' he listened to the final reply and pointlessly nodded his head.

'Yes, goodbye Mr Lincoln'

He replaced the phone and stared out of the window, through the now fading 'blast curtains' to look at the storm clouds gathering on the horizon.

Fate was providing the thunder!

***

Day 7 … Tuesday 3rd May 2016

You've got a Friend in Me!

It was on the fourth evening that Lamb noticed the man. He'd entered the Don Leonne restaurant from the marina and gone straight to the maître d' to show him a card. Lamb feigned disinterest but noticed from his peripheral vision the head waiter nodding in his direction. The man then left and joined a second male standing on the harbour side smoking a hand rolled cigarette. After a brief exchange during which the stub of tobacco was deliberately flicked onto the deck of a £1m yacht, both men looked across at the restaurant and departed separately.

The first part of Lambs plan had worked, now came the hard bit!

There was no point in rushing, so Lamb enjoyed his Brandy and prepared himself for the conflict, he knew would inevitably come. He then paid his bill and strolled out into the warm evening, pausing to covertly appraise the people around him. Approximately ten metres away to his left, he saw the temporary flare of a cigarette being lit. Faint wisps of smoke rose to catch the light from the nearby Michael Kors outlet, before it spiralled up into the warm night air. Now deliberately glancing in that direction, he noticed the sudden movement as the man turned to look into the shop window in feigned innocence.

It was both basic and amateurish and it gave the man away.

The second man, he guessed, would be somewhere to his right, probably at the rear of the shops.

Heading away from the smoker, he walked slowly to the end of the promenade and turned right. He was now temporarily out of sight of the man he knew would be following. Ducking into the shadows he waited tensely for him to arrive. Surprise was on his side and as anticipated, the smell of Golden Virginia preceded the man's arrival by a few seconds. He let him pass before stepping out of the shadows. 'I've been expecting you for several days, so call your buddy and we can talk'

Smoker spun on his heels, surprised but not scared. Launching himself at Lamb he hissed 'It's us that'll do the talking, you just get to listen!' with that he drove his fist into Lamb's ribs then followed it up with an attempted head-butt. He missed the forehead and instead landed a glancing blow to Lamb's left ear.

Lamb gripped the man's shirt and pulled hard, tearing it whilst delivering a savage blow to the smoker's groin with his knee. Then the pent-up fury of recent days took over and he elbowed the man hard in the face. As he watched him crumble, he shouted 'I just want to talk idiot, that's all, just talk!'

During this skirmish, he hadn't seen the second man arriving and although he remembered the kidney punch, he had no recollection of the blows to the head that felled him.

He came to in a cold whitewashed room, tied to a chair with the taste of blood on his lips.

There were now three men standing over him, one scowling through a bloodied face whilst rubbing his groin. Neither of them was ever going to win a beauty pageant and he knew that if this part of the plan went pear shaped, it wouldn't matter if the shirts did find him, he'd probably be castrated or dead!

***

Both shirts were feeling optimistic. They had just been informed by Pontin, that someone with a hard-Scottish accent had telephoned the number in the newspaper article. The male caller was certain, that the fraudster mentioned was the same person he had seen locally. He also said he was one hundred percent sure the man's name was Martin Lamb, which was curious, unless he'd talked to him. Apparently, the observation had been in the Marbella area and no he didn't want to give his own details, but if he saw Lamb again, he'd call back.

Warling was crowing 'What did I tell you my impatient little friend eh? sometimes I'm amazed at my own genius'

Wojtek resisted the weak urge to offer praise 'We'd have found him sooner or later anyway, are we meeting the other two in Marbella?'

'No although they will have been informed of this latest news, it could still be a red herring, so until we confirm it, they will continue enquiries in Fuengerola. Only now they'll be concentrating on the bus stations and taxi ranks' he looked around then lowered his voice 'If we do locate him it will be a joint effort to debrief him' he paused smiling 'Or otherwise … those are our orders'

***

Day 8 … Wednesday 4th May 2016 … 01.27hrs am

Question Time

Lamb tried to speak, but as soon as he uttered a sound, a backhand slap whipped his head sideways 'You'll talk when we say you can and only then … got it?

Lamb didn't acknowledge, there was no point, he could feel blood and saliva running down both his cheek and chin and a tooth felt loose.

The largest of the men leaned forward 'Ok why are you asking around about Frankie Lane? why have you got a photo of him? and what sort of help could some cheating lying toe-rag like you give him?'

He was about to answer, when a vicious kick to the chest sent both him and the chair crashing backwards, wrenching his arms and cracking the back of his head 'Not content with conning old ladies, you want to take Frankie on, you must be bloody stupid'

Temper now overcame the pain and spraying both blood and spittle he yelled at them 'Tell him I can help him get to the UK, That the stuff in the paper about me, was a stitch up! I bet he'll know all about that!'

Arms dragged him back into the sitting position.

'How can you help him and how do we know you're not just trying to cosy up to him, to get out of your own crap?' a rough hand pulled his hair, yanking his head back straining his neck. 'He hates conmen, especially your sort!' again a vicious slap 'How can you help him, tell us, now!'

With the anger still building, Lamb gritted his teeth and spat back 'I told you I'm being framed by the British government because I have something on them!' he glared at the lead protagonist 'Sod it, believe it or not' he sneered angrily 'Please yourself, but you're throwing away the only chance he's got to get him and his wife over to England' he nodded downwards 'There's an sd card in the waistband of my slacks on the right hand side, take it to him, then give me the chance to explain it' he glared again at the man 'Or you could just keep on beating me like the thick sod you are, and get nothing!' he expected a slap but when none came he continued 'Tell him that handled properly this can work for him, but my life is also in danger, so it will have to work both ways!'

One of the men reached down and tore at his waistband, then having retrieved the card leaned forward, his halitosis fouling the air 'This had better not be a con, because if it is your life is definitely in danger! And we'll even turn what's left of your body, over to whoever's on the other end of that phone number!' with that they turned off the lights and locked the door behind them. He was left covered in blood, whilst sitting in a pool of his own urine, the taste of the man's breath still lingered on his tongue.

***

Day 8 … Wednesday 4th May 2016 … 08.10hrs am

It would be a Crime not to!...

Frankie 'Diamond' Lane was tired, not physically but mentally. Aged 74 he was six foot three inches tall, reasonably fit, with chiselled features and long white wavy hair, evocative of a 70s rock star or nightclub owner. He also had a liking for expensive clothing and apart from his navy-blue loafers always wore white. His usual style of long slacks and open neck long sleeved shirt with the cuffs turned up, was always finished off with a chunky gold necklace and bracelet. This was his preferred attire and it suited him; at one time he'd have been considered a 'medallion man' but apart from his wife, no person would ever say so out loud.

Born in the toughest part of London's East end, he'd been a criminal of one sort or another since his teenage years, however his dad had constantly instilled in him the importance of respect and honour. He'd always tried to follow the old underworld code of separating family life from his day job. He'd never dealt in drugs, protection rackets, or prostitution, and violence was a last resort and rarely a means to an end. Breaking into banks and safety deposit vaults were his speciality and over the years he'd forged a mutual respect with both the criminal underworld and the 'Bill' from the Met. Nowadays, criminal standards in the UK and Europe had deteriorated, anything went; armed robbery had replaced tunnelling and safe cracking, violence, drugs and trafficking were the norm. No one wanted the hard work anymore; the skills and respect had gone and he wanted none of i! His world had disappeared a long time ago and now he was retired.

Both he and wife Betty had chosen to live in the sun-drenched hills around Marbella. It had also been a joint decision to take Spanish citizenship. It was a clear commitment to her that his previous life was over and he would do no more jail time. With them, came their long-time acquaintance Billy Cooper, 64, Glaswegian, hard man and fixer. They're relationship had forged a closeness way beyond 'friendship' and Billy had even done jail time with his 'Brother' Frankie.

Since then, other former members of his gang had followed them out to Spain, in a concerted effort to 'change their own ways'

Frankie still retained a hardness; in fact some say that was the reason for his nickname, whilst others said it was his liking for quality gems, maybe even his reputation as being a 'Diamond Geezer'. Either way, he could still summon the services of a very skilled and loyal team of cracksmen and women. Although many were not young, each was still an expert in their own field. He and Betty also knew the gang member's children and if any of those had the special skills he could use, he had only to ask.

However, he'd given Betty a promise not to get involved in crime again and would never break it.

Betty's homely appearance at 5 foot 4 inches tall, slightly built with neat greying hair and thin framed spectacles. belied a fiercely loyal woman, toughened from many years defending her man. A childhood sweetheart, and five years Frankie's junior, she had stood by him during the total of twenty-three years he'd spent behind bars.

And now she was terminally ill!

Frankie knew she wanted to end her days in the East end of London, surrounded by family and friends. However, whilst she could go back anytime, the British Government had refused him permission to return, citing his past record as a reason, and if he couldn't go, she was adamant neither would she!

The truth was, he'd embarrassed the government when they'd tried to convict him on tax evasion charges, several years after his last offence. Through his very competent lawyers and using 'acquired' confidential documents, he'd demonstrated very publicly, that apart from some of their other seedy habits, those who were pursuing him were themselves guilty of the very same practices. The government however, employed their privileged positions and secretive offshore bank accounts, to legally achieve what they accused others of fraudulently doing. It became clear to them very quickly, that if they persisted with the prosecution, it could be very embarrassing for many of their ilk, in the elitist 'establishment' of the capital.

However, they never forgave him. So recently, he'd resorted to appealing in the British newspapers to evoke support and compassion, if only for Betty. After all it had been almost twenty years since his last 'heist' and he had no outstanding warrants. All that was to no avail though, the powers that be stood resolute, even resorting to tarnishing his reputation by inferring an involvement in drug dealing. something that was abhorrent to him, and they knew it! His most recent denial and appeal had also been reported in the local ex-pat papers in Spain, several days ago.

The UK government were using his love for his wife as a weapon of revenge and now he was frustrated, tired and bloody angry!

A knock at the door of his private office brought him back to reality 'Come in Billy'

A stocky man with tattoos and a long-time broken nose, entered, 'Morning Frankie, it's about this Lamb bloke we're holding, there's something not square with him, it's not what we expected!'

Frankie eyed him for a second, Billy's judgement was always sound 'How do you mean not what you expected?'

'Well for a start, we've had a real meaningful conversation with him and left him overnight to sweat, but believe me he's no pushover, he's certainly not like any con-merchant I've ever met. He's saying he's getting stitched up by the British government and that his life's in danger and he's given us one of those memory card things to look at. I mean that's unusual in itself!'

Frankie looked out through the large bay window, across the infinity pool to the terracotta roof tops of the town below, then looked down at the small black object Billy had just placed on the desk. 'Ok Billy, give the Wizz a call and ask him to come over, he knows how to work all this techno stuff, then stand by with our visitor in case I want to talk to him'. He added as an afterthought, 'Billy clean him up, we don't want any 'meaningful conversation' dripping on the marble do we' they both grinned.

Some fifteen minutes later; Sam 'The Whizz' looked up from the laptop screen, where he and Frankie had been watching the contents of the sd card 'It all looks genuine Guv, but I don't have a clue what it's about. I could do some research but even then I might not figure it' he paused thoughtfully, 'I reckon there's more to this story than what's on here and that Lamb geezer must have the key, sorry Frankie'

'It's ok Whizz, tell Billy to bring the Lamb guy up to the back terrace with a couple of the lads, oh and leave me the laptop switched on'

Strong arms grabbed Lamb and dragged him up to the rear terrace. He was then pushed firmly down onto a hard-cold seat, part of a circular marble table set that made up the terrace furniture.

Frankie stared at the 'visitor' noting the bloodied shirt, stained trousers, the now darkening bruise around the closing left eye and the swollen lips 'Sorry you had to suffer that but I'm going through difficult times. If I thought you were using them to try and scam me, well let's just say you wouldn't be sitting there. I needed to know that you weren't just a con merchant, do you understand?' he waited for it to sink in 'So I won't mess with you any more Lamb and I don't want any crap from you either … so … tell me who are you, why you're here and why you think I need your help. Also what's the significance of this memory card' he paused 'And Lamb tell us in words we all understand … ok?' He glanced across the terrace 'Get him a bag of ice for his face Billy, in fact bring us all a gin and tonic as well, Hendricks with cucumber and ice, it doesn't hurt to be sociable' he smiled at the unintended joke and winked at Billy 'Depending on which side of the table you're sat' they all laughed except Lamb.

Lamb explained the events leading up to the present time; Mary's death, the reason for his coming to Spain, how he'd come into possession of the man's phone and subsequent murders of Georgio and Sergio. Finally, he told them of the 'shirts' involvement and the gun he'd seen them with.

Earlier, one of the Frankie's men had gone to Lamb's hotel to retrieve his belongings, so Lamb showed Frankie and Billy the newspaper report regarding the deaths in Nerja. He also explained how he'd seen, in the same newspaper, the article highlighting the British government's refusal, to allow Frankie to return to London with his terminally ill wife. He then outlined how they could mutually help each other, considering his own life was in danger!

'And the card?' Frankie asked, with just a hint of empathy.

Lamb tried to take a sip of his gin and tonic but dribbled most of it due to his swollen lips. Ice and cucumber flopped messily into his lap. Then looking up through his one good eye he spoke quietly. 'I'm going to ask you to really trust me on this Lane … I only want to explain what's on the card to you and your most trusted friend … I'm assuming, that will be the nutter here' he nodded towards Billy 'Because what I'm about to tell you loses its effectiveness with every person who knows. You can explain to the others it's not about distrust' he expected a protest, but none was forthcoming 'Anyway Lane if after I've told you what's on the card and you disagree, you can tell them anyway, you've nothing to lose!'

Frankie looked over at Billy, who raised his eyebrows and shrugged his shoulders in agreement 'Look Lamb I trust my lads and they trust me and they'll do whatever I ask of them 'he smiled, beginning to admire the man's nerve 'There's something about you Lamb, I can't pinpoint it yet, but ok have it your way, and by the way you can bin the 'Lane' it's just Frankie ok? Oh, and the nutter over there, that's Billy and he still isn't sure about you, remember that!' he signalled for the others to go 'Billy get us all another drink, only this time give him a straw he's wasting good Hendricks, no cucumber though …. he doesn't seem to like it'

When all three were settled around the table, Lamb ran them through the images and videos. He explained the irony of the false 'names' and the twisted logic behind the project title 'Bikini' Then he explained the meaning of the documents and how they revealed a plot by the British, American and Iraqi governments to install Weapons of Mass Destruction *'into'* Iraq, in the guise of an Aqua Park redevelopment scheme.

He also detailed the proposed deception in the ordering and delivering of the tubular water slide sections and how the missiles would be concealed inside them, for shipment to Iraq.

Next, he described how he'd found out about the M1003 (MGM-31C) Pershing missiles and their launchers and how he believed they hadn't all been destroyed back in the 80s.

'That alone could cause a massive rift with Russia, and would almost certainly trigger a new arms race! If they've hoodwinked the Weapons Inspectorate over their own WMDs, it's not only hypocritically embarrassing, their credibility disappears too! I mean what else have they been hiding?'

He then went on to explain the reference to the SS-1d Scud missiles 'The real importance of which I'll come to later'

Frankie and Billy looked across at each other, still unconvinced.

Lamb continued, telling them about the intended use of 'Coalition assets' in the form of large military aircraft, to ship the missiles into Iraq;

'Before they're dispatched, the launchers would have their tracks removed and be re-painted in neutral colours. They could then be concealed in the park, disguised as large pumps or generators' He pushed forward his theory 'Who would notice? they could be positioned next to tall dummy filtration tanks, the sort commonly found at such installations. Inside and ready to launch would be the upright missiles, with specialist operators disguised as Hydraulic engineers to easily maintain or fire them. All sites of this kind have restricted access zones so keeping them concealed wouldn't be too much of a problem' he looked at their expressions and pre-empted the response 'Ok so that bit's guesswork …

but I've seen pictures of large aqua parks and let's not forget, the Iraqi's are onside!'

Between occasional shakes of the head, the other two listened patiently sometimes asking for the odd bit of clarification.

'But how does this help us, they could simply deny it' asked Frankie 'After all we're not the most credible witnesses, are we!'

Lamb continued 'Of course they could deny it but it would still be out there, there's too much detail to ignore. Countries would automatically start investigations anyway. Even the Spanish would re-investigate the deaths of the two men back in Nerja and let's not forget the two Yorkshire women. They witnessed the original murder above the cliffs so any publicity would certainly draw them out of hiding. There's no way the shirts or their bosses could trace and silence them before the news broke and it's my betting the shirts haven't even told their superiors about them' he looked up 'But I haven't forgotten' he sucked up some more gin, wincing at the pain from his face. 'Anyway, if just one tiny part of this plot were found to be fact' he cupped his palms then raised his arms and opened them wide 'Boom!' they looked intently at him 'The Israelis would be the first to react, probably going so far as to destroy them! No way would they want intercontinental missiles capable of reaching them, sitting in a hostile country, certainly not Iraq! Their special relationship with the USA and

Britain would break down and in turn that would give their enemies a greater confidence to attack them!'

At the end of each statement he paused, he needed their complete understanding of what he was saying.

'Iran and Syria would receive more nuclear support from Russia, which in turn would spark outrage in the Arabian states and North Africa' he held out his palms in front of him 'Turkey would kick off big time and China too would ignore the west and expand its operations in the South China Seas. Basically, world trust and even NATO would collapse' he paused 'And all of this just on the back of what's on the sd card, it's worse than if they'd actually gotten around to doing it!'

Frankie's eyes narrowed 'How do you mean Lamb?'

Lamb stubbed his finger on the cool marble top 'Look you both need to understand something, this was all about secrecy, it was never meant to be a deterrent. It was to be a means of attacking Iran or Syria only if either managed to obtain nuclear weapons and threatened the supply of oil to the west!' he paused 'It all fits! my own guess is that the heading 'M1003 (MGM-31C) – (SS-1d) Modification Requirements' refers to the Pershings being disguised as old Russian SS-1d Scud missiles, they're not too dissimilar in size or shape. In the event of them ever being discovered, this new coalition would simply accuse Russia of complicity with Saddam Hussein before the Gulf Wars. They'd say they were Russian missiles, that had been sitting there undiscovered for years. The UN weapons inspectors might try to refute it, but remember their visits were always sabotaged anyway. Then they'd be destroyed to hide the actual evidence and finally the coalition could justify its claim of WMDs, it's a winner all round 'he tried a dribbling smile. 'The trouble is someone found out too soon … me'

Billy was the first to react 'Let me get this right; if we use what we know, all hell breaks loose in the world, therefore we daren't use it, and if we daren't use it the knowledge is useless anyway, so what's the point?'

Frankie nodded 'My feelings exactly and at the moment it still seems fantasy land to me'

'Ok I can see what you're getting at' Lamb continued 'By now they must have an idea that I would be very reluctant to use it, because of the chaos and deaths it could cause. They trust me to have a conscience … however' he stopped for emphasis 'They daren't risk calling my bluff … so they kill me, get the card, and it all goes away'

'That still doesn't explain how it helps us' Frankie interrupted

'No disrespect Frankie but your criminal reputation and current situation is the key to this. Basically, once they find out that you know of the plot too, they'll get very worried. They'll see you as a desperate villain with no conscience. In their eyes you're someone who hates them. and will go to any lengths to help his wife, even if it means releasing what's on the card' he tried to smile 'They just don't see you as the 'Mr nice guy' you really are' he put his fingers to his swollen eye and managed a croaky laugh 'Trust me you'll make them very nervous'

'They'd be right about that' interjected Frankie 'I would and anyway from what you just said they'll now try to kill me and Billy as well, thanks for that' he winked at Billy 'Anyway why can't I just use it myself? why do I need you?'

Lamb continued 'I certainly wouldn't joke about it, but yes, until we resolve it, I would expect them to try and kill you Frankie. Not Billy though, as they'll think of him as just some sort of employee. Remember … you can still walk away from this, as at this moment in time they still don't know I'm talking to you!' He let them think about it for a second 'And as for using the info yourself, you can't for the very same reasons as earlier, your reputation and current desperation discredit what you say immediately, I'm a material witness don't forget, and I bring credibility to our partnership, that's our strength. Trust me, it will really scare them and that works to our advantage. To them, we'll be like a double barrelled shotgun, each with a finger on a hair trigger' he smiled at them 'They won't know which of us to target first, get one and the other fires!' he paused to let them absorb what he'd just said 'No they'll have two options, negotiate or kill us all in one go'. He let the impact of what he'd just said sink in 'Currently the last thing they want to do is talk. So, Frankie and Billy, as from the moment you buy into this you are my insurance and I'm yours! We'll then all have to stay alive, and I reckon that would be your department eh Billy' he lowered his tone 'Whilst this may look like we're trying to blackmail the government, we're not. It's about justice for you and Betty Frankie, and revenge for me … I want the bastards that killed Sergio, nothing else … what happens to me afterwards doesn't matter'

'Revenge eh?' Frankie smiled 'I could do with some of that myself' he frowned 'I can't risk getting into trouble here in Spain Lamb, not with the short time Betty's got left' the last words were hushed and fractured 'Any other time …' the sentence faded.

'Frankie, all we're doing is convincing everyone that we mean business, to do that we need to demonstrate, that be they governments or not, trying to kill us is both risky and futile. Don't worry, I do have a plan that I've been working on since I saw the article about you in the paper …' he paused 'I might as well say this now and get it over with' he took a deep breath 'It's complex and it will mean you contacting some of your old colleagues or associates, whatever you call them'

'Friends Lamb, they're called friends' Frankie interrupted 'Go on'

'And ...' he hesitated 'I'll need some drugs ... cocaine will do, in fact quite a large amount of cocaine' he took a deep breath 'About fifty-thousand euros' worth'

Frankie couldn't believe what he'd just heard and stared wide-eyed at Lamb, his voice rose in anger 'Did you hear that Billy? he wants drugs, fifty-grands worth! he stood up and leaned over Lamb 'Just for a minute there I believed you were genuine, what a mug I was! I hate drugs, they're evil and anyway it would just confirm what the British Government have been accusing me of!' he moved his head closer to Lambs 'There's no way I'll risk my freedom or Betty's happiness on drugs! Start explaining Lamb, or we'll throw you to the lions now! In fact, Billy take him away, have a meaningful talk with him and throw him out!'

Lamb rose from his seat 'Frankie listen to me! I asked you to trust me, didn't I? no drugs will be coming anywhere near this place and neither you or your lads will be implicated! he spoke quietly 'But I do need those drugs!' He paused for a second 'And cash I'll need lots of cash, a random number though, let's say thirty-eight thousand euros, that should do it'

Frankie was incredulous 'And cash? do you hear that Billy? he hasn't been here a full day yet and has just asked me for eighty-eight thousand euros in drugs and cash! You know what, this is just one massive con job, get him out of here!'

Billy rose but Lamb held his arm out to stop him 'Alright I know it sounds suspicious but first let me explain why I want it and then you can make a judgement call' he lowered his voice again 'Frankie, what you want isn't going to be cheap, these are governments we're taking on, and anyway you've got the money and you know the end result will be worth it!' Over the next two hours he outlined the part of the plan that involved them, though he deliberately omitted to mention the second part. It was in their own interest not knowing. Finally, he said 'So if you now want out, I'll understand and walk away. Don't worry I'll take my chances, at least I can say I tried'

Frankie and Billy exchanged glances 'Ok Lamb it's beginning to make sense, I think. Maybe this is just too much to fathom in one session, so we'll get you cleaned up and into some nice new clothes. At the moment you stink and make the place look scruffy' he turned to Billy 'Get the doc up here to see to his 'meaningful conversations' then get him measured up and send one of the lads to get him some smart clothes on my account. After that we'll have some food … nothing too solid for you yet eh Lamb' he glanced at Billy 'If I go for this, Lamby here, is never to go anywhere near the drugs or cash without you being right by his side, understood Billy? And at the slightest hint of him wandering off you know what to do!' he turned to Lamb 'Just a precaution until we get to know you better, nothing personal ok?'

Billy nudged his boss 'Seeing as how we're in confessional mode, now might be a good time to tell him about the phone call we made to that number in the newspaper 'What was it, the Serious Overseas Fraud Office or something, never heard of it myself'

'Oh yes I forgot about that' he waited for Lamb to sit again 'What Billy's on about is that before we sort of … met with you down at the harbour, we phoned that number to see what sort of reaction we got … It was certainly different, not the usual 'crimewatchers' stuff, but it does mean they now have an idea where you are! … Maybe we were a tad too hasty eh?'

Lamb smiled 'Not at all, quite the opposite in fact, it also means we now have an idea where they will be!'

Fate was throwing a party!

***

Warling was on his mobile, he looked across at his partner and beckoned him closer 'Yes Mr Pontin I understand, of course we will'

When Wojtek stood next to him he smiled 'That was most interesting Filip, it seems that the last call to Mr Pontin was traced back to a mast, in an area above Marbella, this is a very important clue for us'. He waited for a comment, but as none was forthcoming, he continued. 'The properties in that area are both expensive and exclusive, with most sharing joint security' he was enjoying the showing off 'This leads us to conclude my dear Filip' again a pause 'That it is extremely unlikely, anyone would venture up there, just to make an anonymous phone call, it would be both difficult and pointless' he let the significance of his words sink in.' Which also means that in all probability, the call came from inside one of the villas themselves!' Again he waited for a response … impatiently he continued 'Does it not make you at all curious Filip, as to why anyone with such a luxurious lifestyle, would even bother themselves with some innocuous little article in a giveaway newspaper?'

Wojtek nodded 'Interesting Edmond, so maybe we should find out who lives up there, it could tell us who made the call'

'Exactly Filip, if we did find out who it was, they may give us more information as to Lamb's whereabouts … at the back of my mind though, I know something isn't quite right'. He looked up at the hills overlooking the town 'I think it's time to bring our American friends in, things could start moving very quickly from now on'

***

Mr Churchill allowed himself a faint smile, he'd just received a positive call from Pontin, the head of the secretive CLA. Apparently, his men and the Americans we're closing in on this Lamb fellow. They already knew what was required of them when they did get to him, neither himself nor Mr Lincoln needed to spell that out. The implications of what might happen if any part of this scheme were made public were horrendous. It was more serious than anything else that had happened recently, including the wars in the middle east. The coalition and even NATO were at risk, all because some idiot couldn't keep hold of his documents whilst he went for a piss! It had now become obvious that 'Operation Bikini' could no longer proceed, but that didn't make the information any less dangerous. They certainly couldn't trust one simple scouser to keep quiet about it. Nor could they let him hold the United Kingdom and the USA to ransom. There was no choice … innocent or not he would need to be silenced! Sometimes the sacrifice of an individual was necessary to protect the greater good! However, first he had a phone call to make, if this thing did explode, there was no way it was just going to land in his lap. He picked up the small red phone that was permanently connected to the encryption device. and tapped number 1 on the speed dial, he also pressed the record button 'Hello Mr Lincoln I trust you are well …

Fate was rattling a cage!

***

Day 9 ... Thursday 5th May 2016

Site for Sore Eyes!

Lamb felt better after the food and a good night's sleep. His ribs were sore and his face was still swollen and though he could hardly see out of his left eye, he was satisfied. He had known the beating might happen and considered it a pain worth suffering to get the desired results. After showering and gingerly brushing his teeth, minding to avoid the loose one, he dressed in his new attire of cream Chinos and mint and white striped sports shirt. Then he walked out, directly onto the rear terrace to join Frankie and Billy for breakfast.

'Jesus Billy' grinned Frankie 'thanks to you and the lads, I've now got to have breakfast looking at

this ugly bastard' this time Lamb laughed as well
'Only joking Lamby you ok? I'll arrange for our
dentist to visit as soon as you can open your mouth
properly, she'll sort you out. Now, I discussed your
plan and the options with Billy last night, and as long
as you can guarantee that this won't hurt Betty, I'm
willing to go along with you, I owe those evil sods big
time!'

'Frankie, I'll be absolutely honest with you, I
can't guarantee anything one hundred percent, but if
we follow my plan it'll be pretty damn close. If you
do agree to it, we should go over everything again
later this morning, we haven't got a great deal of time
to play with'

'Ok Lamb, I'll still go along with it, but you'd
better not let me down. By the way I've decided to
stick with your surname, Martin just doesn't do it for
me, bit grammar schoolish, you don't mind that do
you' he didn't wait for an answer 'I'll be doing my
usual routine with Betty today, she wants me to drive
her into town, so you can fill Billy in with the details,
here on the rear terrace. He can brief me during our
usual session later this evening, oh and when I do
introduce you, no mention of any of this to Betty, it
would horrify her. We'll tell her you're an old friend
of Billy's and say you can't handle your drink, that's
not far off the mark anyway'. Both he and Billy
laughed 'Only joking again Lamby she's not daft but
she'll go with that'

'No problem Frankie, there's something I'd like to sort out with Billy anyway, I could also do with a vehicle, that's if you've got one available'

'Be my guest' he nodded in the direction of Billy 'He'll sort it, by the way he's a good man, he was only doing the job he's expert at, any other bruiser might have killed you, he knows how far is enough'

Lamb rolled his tongue over the loose tooth and winced 'I know he is and that's a good thing to have on our side … I think'

Frankie laughed 'I'll catch up with you later' he patted Lamb on the back 'I can't believe you actually came here, asked for cash and drugs, put me on a government hit list and I still trusted you. My god you've got some bottle Lamb, either that or I'm dealing with a complete nutter' he was still laughing as he started to walk away. Suddenly he stopped and turned with a serious expression on his face 'Nearly forgot, one thing puzzles me, how and at what poin,t do we tell them, I know about 'Bikini'?

Lamb studied him, gauging his mood 'We don't tell them directly Frankie, not in an obvious way. We let them assume that you know, until we're ready to confirm it. We'll try to keep them guessing, anyway with the connections they've got, it won't be secret for long'

Again, Frankie laughed 'Ok I somehow knew you'd have an answer, catch you later'

Billy looked at him 'You want to discuss plans Lamb? I'm all ears'

'Thanks Billy, I have the ideas but you've got the experience. I think the shirts will be sniffing round here pretty soon and they're no mugs, so tell the lads to be on their guard as they're pretty ruthless. Initially we need to buy time, after all we've got to organise the drugs and cash.

'The cash is no problem' Billy replied 'Frankie keeps more than that in his safe, the drugs though could take a few days, I'm going to call in some favours, no question asked' he noticed Lambs look of concern 'Don't worry, they'll arrive via a complicated route and Frankie's name won't even get mentioned. Like him, I hate the damn stuff, but I have to keep up to date with my sources, anyway, knowing where it is helps to avoid it.

'That's great Billy, another thing concerning me, is that eventually we'll need some weapons, in fact a couple of specialised bits of kit' before Billy could answer, Lamb held his hands up 'Don't worry Billy we're not going to harm anyone, that's down to someone else. Would getting hold of them be an issue?'

'No problem getting the hardware, but Frankie won't allow weapons here inside the villa ... give me your list anyway. Again, I've got contacts around Spain who'll help out, as for protection we're pretty safe here'

That last sentence would shortly be coming back to haunt him!

***

Down in Marbella, the shirts had ignored breakfast at the hotel and strolled the short distance to the marina. Both were in a positive mood as they settled down into the corner of a café and ordered croissants, fresh orange juice and iced coffee. Then they proceeded to plan their day. First, they needed to pin point the exact location of the mobile communications mast,

Warling retrieved his mobile from the dedicated pocket in his 'Visconti' man bag and made a call. 'Yes got that thank you, I will pass that information on to the Americans when we speak later this morning, Filip and I have some errands to run after breakfast' he paused 'Yes, of course we will Mr Pontin' he then addressed Wojtek 'Our colleagues back home, have pinpointed a more precise location of the call that Mr Pontin received' He pulled out a tourist map from his bag and unfurled it onto the table 'There's a high probability it came from somewhere around here' he circled his finger around the top portion of the map 'The Calle Liszt and Calle Granados area,

'I think it's about time our American friends got on the property ladder Filip' he speed-dialled a number on his mobile 'Ah Mr Harkant, I trust we haven't disturbed your breakfast, no? good, I have some information for you' He waited patiently for the reply 'See you in an hour then? fine I've a good feeling about today'

***

Following Frankie's departure, Tommy his standby driver, took Lamb and Billy out into the Sierra hills behind Marbella. The three men were looking for a particular type of building, somewhere remote but accessible by vehicle, it also needed to be uninhabited but not too decrepit, more important than the structure of the building was its surroundings and the direction it faced.

Billy looked across at Lamb pouring over the Michelin map 'Look Lamb that's the fourth one we've seen and personally I can't find fault with either of the last two, I mean, what if there is no such building around here … what then?'

Lamb smiled 'Ok Billy I can see where you're coming from, but until we do find it I can't really explain why it has to have certain features, but be patient for a little while longer' he paused 'If we can't find one with the exact spec but near enough, we'll convert it. Okay Tommy, let's go look at the next one, swing left 50 yards up' Some two hours later, Lamb put his hand up 'Hold it Tommy! reverse up to that track on the left we just passed, I think I might have spotted what we're looking for' he glanced down at the map, reading the contour lines as he'd been taught in the army, then looked up to confirm their surroundings 'Fingers crossed this could be it. Pull over behind that small hillock Tommy, we'll walk the rest of the way' Once parked up, they climbed out of the white Range Rover and rambled slowly towards the front of a little white-washed building, 150 yards ahead of them. Lamb was constantly stopping to look at the surrounding hills, all the while measuring angles by zigzagging either side of the track.

'If this place is unoccupied it'll do us fine' he said going around to the rear of the building. He studied the features of the long sweeping valley that meandered its way towards the western horizon. Peering round the side of the building to check the route they'd just come from. he again turned and studied the valley, He looked at Tommy and pointed to some rocks two hundred and fifty yards away and half way up the valley wall to the left 'Tommy you go over to that bunch of rocks up there and crouch down' he turned slightly right 'Billy you do the same, by that clump of trees on that rocky outcrop, two-hundred yards away on the other side' As they set off, he walked back towards the front of the building and then up the track towards the parked Range Rover. One-hundred yards on, he turned, shading his eyes from the glaring sun and looked out towards his two companions, noting the time on his watch. It was just after midday, so he made a mental calculation, then called Billy from his mobile,

'Billy what time do reckon sunset will be in this place? I'm reckoning around nine o'clock judging by the last few days' he listened to the reply 'Ok, agreed but someone will have to come back to confirm it, so far though, this looks as good as we're going to get'

He then returned to the rear of the finca and made his way out to a curious Billy and Tommy. They spent the next two hours going over his plan multiple times. The building was an old finca that had been used as a goat herders' shelter, before being abandoned many years ago. Inside, the floor was bottle strewn and against the back wall stood a rickety set of drawers, that at one time had multiple uses: All confirmed by the many stains and rusty camping stove on the top. Whatever light there was, came in through the small solitary glassless window to the front, which could only be looked out of by standing on the rusty metal bedframe. The front door was just hanging on by its one remaining broken hinge and Lamb explained to Billy the need to have it sympathetically repaired, with the addition of a new lock. One that could only be used in a particular way. Also, inside he gave Billy the dimensions and location for another vital project. Then going around the outside of the building he explained further modifications.

'All this needs to be made to look as though it's been that way for years. We want it secure but not obviously so, and it needs to be done unseen by anyone' he looked back at their parked vehicle 'And this is the last time that Range Rover comes anywhere near the place, it's important that no connection can be made to us, that's why I had it parked up behind the rocks. What do you reckon Billy, is this job going to be a problem?'

'No, it's a piece of cake Lamb, Bert one of our lads used to be an all-round bricklayer and carpenter, came in handy on some jobs. He could remove or build a false wall or break through and repair a bank door and no one would ever be the wiser, we'll get him flown out in the morning and he'll be on the job tomorrow night'

He'd previously noticed that the guard in Frankie's gate house used crayons to chart the comings and goings of visitors and this had given him an idea. He'd borrowed' a red one and now used it to draw a small red circle on the map, pinpointing the exact location of the building they'd just left.

It was a small but vital detail of his plan

Half an hour after arriving back from his 'shed hunting', Lamb ate the salmon quiche and salad that was waiting in the room Frankie had allocated him. He then bathed his bruises and put on his RayBan's, after all he didn't want his wounds to alarm the locals. Taking Tommy with him he set off for a walking tour of the area, partly for exercise and partly to familiarize himself with the lay of the land. His left leg was stiff and aching from the rough treatment he'd received, but his bruised eye was beginning to open and all things considered he felt reasonably good. 'I don't know about you Tommy, but I reckon we could be in for some rain later, but no bother, with luck it'll hold off long enough for you to show me who's who and what's what around here. I need to be able to spot anything out of the ordinary'

Fate was already steering the 'who's who and what's what' towards them ... a deadly 'out of the ordinary' collision was inevitable!

***

Lyndon Harkant and Jaycee Cropfeld were feeling smug, since their arrival in Spain, the information flow regarding Lamb's whereabouts had been coming in at a steady rate. It didn't matter whether or not it was entirely due to the 'American' presence, in their minds they were the worlds experts. As Lyndon once put it 'The Brits just spend too much time chasin' their own butts'

Warling had requested their presence in Marbella to brief them about the latest call between him and Pontin. He'd explained how someone had called in anonymously with a positive identification on their quarry. However, as Lamb would recognize the two British guys, Warling asked if they, the

133

Americans, could have a nose around properties just north of Puerto Banus. To see if there were any clue as to where the call could have come from. They were to pose as agents looking for an exclusive property on behalf of an American millionaire client, whilst trying to find out the names of those who already lived in the area.

Even Jaycee could see nothing wrong with that plan.

Warling had also voiced his suspicions about the call 'It doesn't tally, the people up there live in their own private bubbles and it's a totally different world to the one we know. It is absolutely out of character for them to be interested in the type of newspaper article that Lamb featured in'

At the first opportunity, the Americans visited 'Gable and Knight Exclusive Properties' in Marbella's old town and enquired about the area they were interested in. There were three possibilities, two already empty and one which was still occupied on Calle Liszt. Gerald the agent made calls to arrange the viewings.

'Ok sorted, I can take you to the empty properties at one pm then onto the final one around three pm is that alright?'

It was agreed, so Harkant made a call from his own cell phone, but after getting no response, he left the following message …

'Hi Warling, we got lucky, there's a place we're gonna view right in the area that interests us, we haven't asked about names yet but it won't be too hard once we've got the agent eating out of our hands, talk later'

After lunch they returned to Gable and Knight 'Let's do this Jaycee, see if we can't find a Lamb to slaughter' He gave the estate agent his most charismatic smile 'Ok Gerald show us some classy bricks, and we want gold, gold taps, gold chandeliers in fact we want as much gold as you can muster buddy, you lead and we'll follow in our own vehicle, that ok' It wasn't a question.

They smiled and waved, as Gerald climbed into his silver Touareg and drove out toward the hills, his imagination already spending the huge commission.

The first villa they looked at was a vast marble edifice, available for a mere five point seven million euros. Gerald showed them around, expertly flitting from room to room, taking great pleasure in highlighting the pre-requisite chandeliers, as well as the nine bedrooms and two swimming pools, one of which was indoors. Slowly the two Americans teased the information they wanted from him 'I mean our client wouldn't want to be living next to a Columbian drug baron' Harkant joked 'He doesn't appreciate being woken up by sirens in the early hours' he held his hand to his mouth and looked around in mock conspiracy 'He seriously needs his beauty sleep, unlike yourself' he winked

Flattered Gerald responded 'I don't normally discuss the other residents, especially if they are on our books, but as it's not yourselves that will be living here 'I don't really see the harm' After giving them various names and nationalities he paused and laughed 'There is one elderly English couple, a Mr and Mrs Lane who live just off the next street, really nice they are and certainly not Columbian drug barons!' he laughed again 'Nothing could be further from that, but it is funny, and this is only a silly rumour' he paused.

'Go on stop teasing us, out with it' Jaycee chimed in, he was the lesser patient of the two.

Gerald edged closer 'Well it's just a little spicy titbit really' he lowered his voice to add mischief and drama to his words 'It's gossiped, and I'm sure that's all it is' he leaned even closer towards Harkant 'That the husband Frankie Lane used to be a London gangster, way back in the old days, but I personally find it hard to believe. They've lived here permanently for quite some time and a nicer couple you couldn't wish to meet. It does though add to the somewhat romantic myth, that Marbella is full of exotic criminals'

The second property, at six point two million euros, was a total contradiction to the first. Just as vast but apart from the gold fixtures, everything else was pure white! Walls, ceilings, marble floors and even the furniture.

Gerald explained 'The owners were so called Catholics but have returned to Venezuela after the currency there crashed, it virtually wiped them out. So, your client could pick up a bargain and …' he paused to ensure he'd got their full attention 'There's even a fully paid up berth with a yacht called the 'Samaritano Blanco' moored at it, all thrown in for good measure'

The third property, at three point five million euros, was home to a middle-aged French couple who intended to relocate to Cannes. Following their script, Harkant and Cropfeld managed to tease out of them a few more names of their neighbours, then thanked them for the viewing before going outside to confer with Gerald.

'Thanks buddy you did us proud, we'll send the brochures to our client along with the video links, we'll then be in touch with you as soon as he makes a decision. He's currently away for a couple of months so it could be a little while' he shook the smiling Gerald's hand 'Anyway, we're gonna have a look around this area to get a feel for it, so thanks again and hopefully we'll be in touch sooner rather than later' they shook hands and watched as the Touareg cruised out of sight'

Climbing into their Jeep, Harkant smiled at his friend 'Come on Jaycee let's see what else we can discover'

Two hundred yards away and walking towards them, they could see two men, one of whom seemed to be limping slightly, Harkant took out his cell phone and brought up 'images'. Hardly believing his luck he scrolled to the one he was interested in, enlarged it and showed it to his partner.

***

Lamb had seen the Cherokee, coming out of the drive 200 yards ahead of them, however, there was nothing unusual in that, as it was the type of vehicle you'd expect to see in the area. When it drove past them, Lamb only got a cursory look at the occupants, due mainly to the tinted glass. He could see it wasn't the shirts so it didn't set off any mental alarms 'The locals look friendly enough Tommy, recognise them?'

'No mate, that villa is up for sale, so I'd expect to see strangers coming from it. There's a couple more for sale around here as well, reckon it's the world economy or something. You won't see any 'for sale' boards though, people don't drive by window shopping, not at those prices'

They didn't notice the Cherokee turning round to come up behind them and Lamb only reacted as it slowed down to pull alongside.

Too late, they saw the gun in the driver's hand and the seriousness of the situation registered!

The driver spoke quietly 'Don't try and be smart, just walk over here and climb into the back' he indicated the rear door with the barrel of the gun. 'Or you could try running, in which case you'll die on the spot' he grinned 'Not much of a choice I know, but hey, it is a polite warning' the voice was mid-western and the words were calm and measured, the lack of aggression intensifying the threat. He glanced in both directions, making sure no other vehicles were approaching, then pointed the silenced weapon at Tommy 'You first ok, gently, no sudden moves, good, now you Lamb' he smiled as Lamb reacted to his name 'Yeah sure we know who you are, you've caused quite a stir back home'

Lamb guessed that he meant America and inwardly cursed at his failure to anticipate the men, who were now in control of his life.

'Tommy has got no part in this, he hasn't a clue what it's all about, so let him walk ok'

'Lamb, whoever this Tommy boy is, he's not our problem, so don't worry, we have no quarrel with him' he looked at Tommy 'We can hardly have you running straight back to where you just came from, can we? once we get some distance from here you can walk' he turned to Lamb 'You just worry about yourself ok' his voice firmed 'Now I want both of you to hand me your cell phones, then sit on your hands' he waited until they'd complied 'There now, isn't that cosy, just sit quietly and don't upset Jaycee here next to me' he nodded towards the gun in Jaycee's hand 'He's forever having accidents and that nine mil's got a very sensitive trigger' both Americans emitted a slight laugh.

Whilst Jaycee covered both prisoners, Harkant retrieved a Michelin map from the glovebox and climbed out of the Jeep, spreading it over the bonnet he made a call to Warling 'Hi Harkant here, we're giving a lift to someone you might like to talk to, so how about we arrange a meet' the arrogance in his voice was unmistakable.

Lamb listened as both parties discussed a suitable location, it was decided that Harkant's team would make its way down to Calle Verdi then turn north to follow the dirt road, that meandered its way into the tree covered hills. The Michelin map indicated a Molino de Madera 'timber mill' about fifteen miles into the forest, so Warling and Wojtek would set off immediately and meet them there in about an hour. Although the track was barely wide enough for two vehicles to pass, they made reasonable time and after a particular winding section some ten miles into the hills, Harkant stopped the Jeep. On Lamb's side of the track was a near vertical hillside, on the other was an almost shear drop of thirty-five metres.

'Okay Tommy fellow, end of the journey, its time you jumped ship, I reckon it'll take a good four hours for you to get home from here … now listen carefully, when you get out, walk to the rear of the wagon and stand there facing downhill. Once we've gone, you can take a hike, got that? ok Jaycee let Mr Tommy out please'

Tommy started to protest 'I'm not leaving Lamb here if he stays so do I'

Jaycee pressed the barrel of his gun tight against Tommy's forehead 'You don't get to make the choices, you get to obey ours, does this make it clear enough'

Lamb turned 'Tommy no way, you go back it'll be alright, honest, I know what these guys are after and I'll just give it to them, so please mate, you go'

'Okay Lamb' he looked directly at Harkant 'You hurt him and we'll track you down whatever it takes' he leaned across towards Harkant hoping to infer menace but again the pistol touched his head 'See you soon Lamb' he climbed out of the Jeep and stood in the narrow space between the vehicle and the small section of Armco barrier that protected the drop. He glanced at Lamb one last time then turned and walked towards the rear of the Jeep.

He'd just taken his third step when a powerful hand caught him between the shoulder blades and pushed.

Lamb watched in horror as his companion stumbled over the barrier and fell into the void, the unnatural scream searing the event into his memory. Numbness and hatred filled him and he watched in disbelief as Jaycee calmly took some photos of the view with Tommy's mobile phone, wiped it clean of fingerprints, then tossed it over the edge to join the broken torso down below.

'The depths to which some people will go, just to get a decent photograph' Harkant gave Lamb a warning smile as he activated the rear child locks 'Wouldn't want you falling overboard, now would we'

Lamb realised the pointlessness of yelling at them, it was obvious they were devoid of any conscience. These were ruthless killers, specially selected to carry out the dirtiest types of mission. He also knew that he needed to escape, before they were joined by the shirts. Once all four of them were together he'd have no chance. He started by engaging them in conversation, probing for their immediate intent.

'I know what you're after but you don't think I'd be crazy enough to carry it on me do you, if you did, it makes you sort of dumb doesn't it' he waited for some kind of reaction but what followed was minimal, Harkant glanced in his rear-view mirror and 'Jaycee' just stared menacingly over his gun. 'There's more than one copy anyway and if I don't get home by nightfall, you all get to read about it in tomorrow's Tel-Aviv tabloids. Somehow I don't think that'll please your boss ... talking of which I wonder how Mr Pontin is?'

Light rain spattered on the windscreen as they climbed higher into the forest and mist played ghosts amongst the pine trees on the mountain peaks.

The Cherokee turned into the deserted timber mill; its usefulness having long ago been replaced by the advance of modern forestry techniques. Several rickety wooden buildings, now green with mildew, formed an escort to the once proud sawing shed, whilst tall mounds of sawdust. defied gravity, glued by the covering of waterlogged Sphagnum moss. Harkant drove around the back of what had once been office, the windows of which were now boarded up. He parked and then walked back to ensure the vehicle couldn't be seen from the road and returned to the vehicle where Jaycee was guarding Lamb.

Switching off the child locks, Harkant was the first to speak 'Okay Lamb climb out slowly, no sudden moves. You might start thinking about what you're going to tell us, once the others arrive, no point dragging it out' he surveyed their surroundings 'Keep an eye on him Jaycee I'm going for a mooch around the saw shed over there, could be its got everything we need' he winked meaningfully in Lamb's direction.

Jaycee nodded then turned to Lamb 'Make for the that entrance over there' he indicated a partially open door in the office block 'And walk very slowly'

Lamb complied, and entered a square room with a disarray of desks and cabinets. Shafts of daylight coming through the now warped timbers of the shuttering highlighted the controlled frenzy of midges; homely it was not.

That didn't matter to Lamb, he didn't want homely, he wanted opportunity and this was dammed near as perfect as he could expect, given the circumstances!

He was ordered to stand against the far wall with his hands on his head.   Meanwhile, Jaycee had positioned himself fifteen feet away, so he could look through a gap in a shuttered window facing the track they'd just driven up 'Don't get any silly ideas Lamb, we don't want to kill you' he smiled 'Yet, but we will if we have to' he waved his gun hand at the midges 'Goddam bugs'

Lamb copied the motion of wafting the midges away, then started scratching as if bitten, he deliberately wanted his captor to get used to seeing movement in his peripheral vision. When he took his chance, he would need every millisecond he could buy, that and the element of surprise, could just make the difference between life or death.

After a few minutes, as the American impatiently waved his arms again whilst casting a quick glance through the shutter, Lamb hurled himself towards the nearest wall in an adrenalin fuelled shoulder charge. As expected, the boards were rotten and pushed straight through the rusty nails. He carried, on not daring to look back as a bullet dug itself into a pine tree to his left. A second shot from behind cracked near to his head, but by now he was among the trees and hurtling downhill on a mattress of pine needles. More shots followed and he could hear an engine cough into life. He stumbled and crashed into a tree, badly bruising his arm and tearing his shirt open in the process. Ignoring the pain, he changed direction, still downhill but to the right, away from where he knew the track to be. Another shot cracked through the branches off to his right but the sound was further away. He figured it must have been Jaycee firing, the other American must be trying to cut him off, somewhere along the track.

When no more shots came for a few minutes, he dared to stop and look back. He took deep breaths, to steady his heart rate and control the sound of his breathing, then opened his mouth to better listen. It was a technique he'd learned in the army, during exercises in the forests of the Hertz mountains of Germany. The rain had stopped and the only sounds were the occasional droplets falling from the branches. There was no sound of a pursuer among the pines but off to his left he could just discern the distinctive growl of the slowly driven Jeep. Then he heard the second engine, it was revving faster and getting louder, so he figured this must be the shirts coming up the track. No matter; it would be dusk soon and in this dense forest he was relatively safe. It wouldn't be too easy to get back to Frankie's however; whilst they may not have known the exact property he and Tommy had walked from; the Americans obviously knew which area. It wouldn't be too hard for them to work out the rest. Knowing they'd be waiting for him; he took the decision to remain where he was for the night. Darkness may be a cloak to hide under but it also hid his pursuers, far better to use the daylight to get back. They would now be taking it in turns to watch for him but even so, they'd still be tired in the morning. He on the other hand would bed down under the pine needles and try to get some sleep.

He needed a plan, maybe fate would play a part.

***

Warling's emotions were working overtime, his frustration at having been crowed at by the colonial cousins, who had caught Lamb after only a few days, had been replaced, by the pleasurable anticipation of the joint interrogation. Then anger had returned to target the fools who had lost him. But now limited pleasure was creeping back, he was sure he knew where Lamb was heading.

'There's no point in trying to catch him in this forest, he could be anywhere. However, I'm pretty certain I know where he'll head for' he paused relishing the moment, this was his theatre, the other three were merely his audience, he turned to his companion 'Philip if you would be so kind as to fetch me the English newspaper from the back seat of our vehicle'

Harkant contained himself, they had lost Lamb and this was payback for his own earlier gloating 'Ok Warling lay it on thick, we deserve it, but mind you observe the limits, me and Jaycee here aren't exactly in good humour'

Taking the paper off Wojtek, Warling opened it up on the bonnet of the X5 'It was an article I spotted back in Nerja, the significance of which escaped me until today'. He pointed to the story in question, on page three 'Here it is, it's about an ex-gangster from London who's trying to get back to the UK because his wife is poorly' he was dragging it out 'Now look at the area where he lives' he used his finger his to indicate a particular sentence 'Above Puerto Banus' coincidently where the phone call came from and … coincidently where you picked Lamb up' he let it sink in 'we just need to find the house'

Harkant interrupted, happy to cut short the conceit 'The estate agent Gerard … Gerald … or whoever, mentioned him, we just never got a chance to connect it, what with picking up Lamb and all. We do know his address though, so what say we have two of us watching the villa, whilst the other two keep watch on the road up here. We could split our teams, that way we get to share any incoming intel as it happens' he waited until all nodded their assent. 'Jaycee you go with Wojtek and cover the track, I reckon the best spot will be on the lower side of that small bridge over the gully we crossed. I'll travel with Warling he, down to the house, between us we should have it covered' he stopped 'We all know the end game right?'

Day 10 … Friday 6th May 2016

If you go down in the woods today!

Back in London Mr Churchill was back inside his secure zone and on his red phone again, only this time he'd' instigated the call. 'Ah Mr Lincoln how are you today, I trust you've been fully briefed about your agents misfortune' he waited hoping his smugness wasn't transmitting too obviously across the airwaves. 'No I don't believe that is correct, we passed everything we knew about him to your people, if they then underestimated him that was their own failing, perhaps you should have words with them'. The sound of Lincoln's irritation at least tempered the overall fear he'd felt, since Operation Bikini had been compromised. 'I'd like to put forward a rather good suggestion that Mr Pontin has come up with. Namely that we ask our Iraqi friends to supply us with' he paused again 'With … how shall I put it … a certain expendable asset' he let the last part sink in 'Look I'll come straight out with it, we know of course that

Lamb spent some time in Iran during the Shah's regime … well what if there was a long standing grudge against him. It's common knowledge that such things do exist. Maybe something the Iranians had just recently trawled up, I'm sure there are skeletons hidden'. he listened to the reply 'Well it would certainly deflect any accusations of our own complicity' he waited for a response that didn't come, so he continued 'I said expendable as it obviously wouldn't work if the er … 'Lone Wolf' so to speak, were able to talk about it afterwards. Of course, the plan would need to be fleshed out but that would be down to our respective departments and of course we would also need to approve any plan first' again he waited … 'Yes, I thought so too … your first impression is the same as mine … I personally think it definitely merits consideration' the smugness was gone now honours were even 'Yes and you too Mr Lincoln shall we say same time tomorrow'

Fate had parted the clouds, but for how long.

***

Lamb awoke feeling surprisingly fresh considering the circumstances of the previous day. Once he'd dug himself into the pine needles, the adrenalin had drained from his body sending him into a deep slumber. He had no fear of the forest, having spent much of his childhood sleeping in dens, whilst exploring the ancient Leicestershire woodlands around the farm where he'd lived. He'd listened to the creatures of the night, the Owls, Foxes, Badgers and numerous other nocturnal mammals, whooping and scuttling around him but they were just curious about the interloper and meant him no harm, unlike the two-legged creatures outside the forest, waiting for him to break cover. No, if anything disturbed his sleep, it was the reoccurring flashbacks of the people who had died because of his stubborn refusal to hand over a stupid phone. Now only retribution could dull that ache.

He stretched, easing the stiffness from his muscles, then paused, holding his breath, absorbing the surroundings. Remembering the horror of the previous day, he fought to bring his mood down to a controlled rage. They the aggressors had played their cards, no quarter was to be expected, so be it, nor would it be given, He now needed to get back to Frankie's, it was almost certain he'd have people out looking for him and Tommy, though by now they might already know of Tommy's fate. What concerned him, was that no one would be alert to the presence of the Americans or how Tommy had really died.

Before settling down for the night, he'd realised that when he awoke, he'd probably be disorientated. So again, using experience from his army days, he'd torn some bark from the trunk of the nearest pine tree, on the side where he knew the track to be. He now chose that direction and cautiously made his way down towards the edge of the forest. After a couple of hours, he came to a break in the treeline. Peering through it, he could see the track winding its way down some seven kilometres, towards the villas set in the hillsides above Puerto Banus. A gully now lay between him and the next part of his journey, which meant he would have to travel over a small bridge on the track itself. This was something he hadn't considered, if there was going to be a trap, this was the ideal location.

He crept forward to peer through the fallen branches and pine needles at the very edge of the forest. Even before he saw it some fifty yards away, he could hear the Jeep's engine ticking over noisily as it fought to drive the air conditioning. It was parked facing uphill on the lower side of the bridge.

Whilst their vehicle remained in its present position, he knew he had little chance of getting past the occupants, whom he discerned to be Blue eyes and Jaycee the American. He also doubted it would turn and go down the hill any time soon. That left him with no alternative but to draw it over the bridge and back up the track, and for that he needed a plan.

Moving cautiously and staying some ten yards into the forest. he retreated back the way he'd come, then turned east to follow the track uphill until he came to a sharp left-hand bend. He exited the trees and stealthily crept forward to look around the corner and back downhill towards the Jeep some three hundred yards away. He could just make out the two occupants and the lack of condensation and smoke from the exhaust suggested the engine had now been switched off. That was a bonus, it would delay their response by a few vital seconds! Wasting no time, he began to collect the largest logs and fallen branches to lay across the track whilst constantly checking for movement from the vehicle.

After an hour he was satisfied with his efforts, the interlocking branches were now a barrier two feet high and arranged at an angle of forty-five degrees. The furthest point of the barrier aimed away towards a steep drop on the right-hand side of the track. Covered in fresh foliage torn from the pines, it wasn't perfect, but it was the only plan he had and he hoped the pursuers aggression, combined with their lack of local knowledge would do the rest.

He moved back into the forest and made his way downhill until he was fifty yards from the bend and two hundred and fifty yards from the killers. Taking a few deep breaths to steady his heart rate, he calmly walked out from the trees and onto the track in full view of them. At first, they seemed to not notice him but then he saw movement in the vehicle as the passenger door flew open. Feigning surprise, he turned and ran back along the track towards his waiting ambush, hoping that whoever was giving chase would now decide to get back in the Jeep to pursue him. The revving of the engine confirmed he'd judged the distance exactly right and now spurred by adrenaline, he raced for the bend. It was going to be tight but just as he was out of sight he leapt into the woods to his left, turned and ran back down through the trees towards the bridge.

***

It was Wojtek who spotted Lamb first and as he opened his door and jumped out, Jaycee behind the wheel screamed at him 'Get back in, we'll catch him up' and started the engine, but his companion was already drawing his gun and running up the track. He floored the accelerator and the wheels spun furiously, kicking up dirt and stones as the large 4 x 4 juddered into action. Ignoring Wojtek as he passed him and with the engine screaming, Jaycee and Jeep hurtled forward into the bend and the waiting barrier. Too late his mind comprehended the situation and with his foot now hard on the brakes, the vehicle crashed into the obstacle forcing the steering towards the void on the right. Man, machine and barrier then plunged down the steep incline through the trees towards the floor of the ravine a hundred feet below. A third of the way down the Jeep hammered into a large pine tree. The airbag exploded into Jaycee's chest and as he wasn't wearing his seatbelt, it forced him upwards to ram his skull into the top of the windscreen. He never heard the fiery explosion that killed him.

High above, Wojtek froze in perverse curiosity.

A few days later, the police would find a 9mm gun on Jaycee Cropfeld's burnt remains and assume some vague connection between his death and Tommy Jarvis's. However, both fatalities would be independently recorded as accidental.

Lamb heard the explosion behind him but felt no emotion, there'd be time for that later on. For now, he needed to get over the bridge and into the trees beyond. He was half way over the bridge when the first shot ricocheted off the rocky track near his feet, the second went higher to the right and he knew one of the killers wasn't injured and was now coming after him. The distant sound of the shot was different to the American's previous attempts, so he could assume it was Blue eyes now in pursuit. This wasn't the time or place to dwell on it though, he was almost there! Putting in a final effort, he ran into the pines, the downhill slope giving him uncontrolled momentum, causing him to fall forward. Tumbling over for thirty yards, he eventually crashed into a pile of timbered logs. He recovered his senses quickly and after some minutes dared a glance back. Just visible on the trail he could make out a lone figure, standing now with a mobile phone to his ear. They were probably going to wait for him to break cover further down, so he changed direction, this way he'd emerge from the forest further west and head for the coast where Freddie's lads could pick him up. Slackening his pace after an hour, he finally stopped and waited until he was sure no one was following, then took stock of his situation.

He was both hungry and thirsty and knew that whilst he could manage without food, fluids were important. The huge amount of adrenalin he'd used had further drained him and he knew that just the thought of water would soon turn into a craving. He wasn't injured, apart from some minor cuts and bruises, and he could now see reasonably well from his swollen left eye, but he felt and looked a mess! His shirt was torn and pine forests not being the cleanest of locations to run about in, filthy! However, considering it was only the day before when he'd had a gun pointing at his head and the prospect of torture and death virtually a certainty, he wasn't too upset!

He now considered the explosion he'd heard and hoped for Sergio's and Tommy's sake, that some form of retribution had now befallen his enemy, if not then it soon would, this was just the beginning!

***

Frankie looked more concerned than Billy had seen in a long while, in fact the last time he'd been this tense, was when he'd got the news about Betty.

'We'll find them Boss I've put the word out; we've got people all over the area scouting for them' at the back of his mind though he wasn't as confident as he'd tried to sound. If Lamb and Tommy had been taken, they could be anywhere, these were professionals they were dealing with.

'Ok Billy but I want to know the second you hear anything understood? and send a couple of lads down to the harbour, in case there's a boat involved!'

'Good idea Boss, I'll arrange it now'

Frankie rose from the table; he was worried not only for Tommy and Lamb but for Betty. She suspected something, after all Tommy Jarvis normally took her to the doctors on a Friday morning, had done for the last six months, so when Billy picked her up with no real explanation, she'd asked her husband why. He knew she hadn't believed his feeble answers, she'd always been able to see through him, especially when he was trying to protect her. Now like a naughty school boy, he'd been summoned into their private suite to 'tell the truth' she'd even used his Sunday name 'Francis', and now 'Diamond Geezer Lane' had turned to putty.

He emerged two hours later, suitably admonished but with an enormous feeling of pride and love for his wife.

She'd told him off for trying to conceal the facts from her 'Of course I knew you were up to something, after all I've known Billy for so many years, I probably remember more of his friends than he does, and I've never heard of this Lamb fellow'

He'd offered to stop all this business with Lamb and the British government but she would have none of it.

'No, you won't Francis Lane! I don't care if we don't get to London, they've treated you terribly and you are my husband! what they do to you, they also do to us as man and wife! yes I know you've not always been a saint but you have paid your debt in full! If you want to fight them then we do it together, understood? furthermore when Mr Lamb turns up I also want to speak with him, is that clear?'

The hardest part was explaining the disappearance of Tommy, but again she amazed him with her compassionate strength.

'Get his wife Judy up here to the villa, where she'll have company, I can tell her the truth, you men treat us women as weak but we only seem that way when we don't have the facts of what's going on. Now what are you waiting for, haven't you got things to be getting on with'

***

After two hours of descending through the trees, Martin Lamb finally emerged at the rocky gorge of the Rio Verde, where a torrent of melt water rushed noisily towards the coast and the Mediterranean Sea. He cupped his hands to greedily drink the refreshing ice-cold liquid that tasted of pine, then splashed his face to rinse the dirt and fatigue away. It was another hour and a half before he reached an empty restaurant and whilst downing two large Magno Brandy's he explained to the barman that he'd fallen over whilst walking in the forest. Eventually, he persuaded the man to let him use the phone and rang Frankie to get him home.

The effects of all the previous adrenalin bursts now piled in and a wave of total exhaustion overcame him, he now not only looked like hell, he felt like hell.

However, others had knocked on the Devil's door!

***

Day 11 … Saturday 7th May 2016

Comes a tall dark Stranger!

It was breakfast down at the harbour and Filip Wojtek previously devoid of serious emotion, was quietly describing the death of Jaycee Cropfeld to Lyndon Harkant and Edmond Warling. 'It was unimaginable! Lamb knew exactly what he was doing! What happened wasn't the actions of a scared man, what I saw yesterday was someone acting coolly and calmly whilst committing murder' he looked at the others to see if it registered 'Jaycee totally screwed up by misjudging him'

Warling frowned at his companion. He'd always known of his insensitivity but seeing the expression on the American's face opposite, he knew immediate restorative action was needed! He intervened to avert a violent confrontation. 'Ignore Filip, he had a bad day yesterday, he means no disrespect to Jaycee or yourself'

Harkant snorted, he'd just lost his partner 'So tell him to wind it in! I don't do that crap, not now, not tomorrow not ever ok! That damn limey just got lucky, it won't happen next time' the slang reference to Lamb's nationality whilst in his present company totally eluded him.

When they'd picked up Wojtek, the flames from the Jeep were still intense. The sound of Jaycee's 9mm ammunition cooking off, mixed with the crackle of timber, added even more menace to the inferno. Quite a few trees were now on fire, sending a towering column of smoke and steam above the forest canopy. Responding to it, the emergency services raced to the scene, fearful of an impending ecological disaster. Faced with the possibility of being seen in the vicinity, by the approaching police and fire fighters, coming up from the town below. They drove uphill, away from the sirens and along the track, taking the long way around.

This inadvertently helped Lamb to return to Frankie's villa unseen

***

Albazi Hashimi walked towards the passport control booth at Malaga airport, having just arrived on the Qatar airlines flight from Doha. Two days previously he'd flown from Baghdad into the small gulf state, on the first step of his deadly mission.

Originally a citizen of Iran; having been born in the northern city of Tabriz, he'd fled with his mother to Turkey during the 1979 revolution. She'd just watched his father being executed; for being a Colonel in the 'Guard de Javadan', the Shah's Imperial troops, based in the Lavizan, district of Teheran. She also died when Albazi was 20, so he moved to Iraq, to help fight against the Islamist regime currently subjugating the people of his homeland!

Now in his late 40's, Albazi was well-known as a cold hearted, outspoken opponent, of the current rulers of Iran and this opinion helped him survive Saddam Hussain's own reign of repression.

Following the coalition invasion of Iraq, he'd been recruited by them to assist the new interim ruling party. They wanted him to weed out and terminate members of Hussain's 'Iraqi Intelligence Service (ISS), Directorate 4', believed responsible for assassinations both in Iraq and abroad.

He'd now been approached by the British again and tipped off about an Englishman, currently living in Spain. They'd inferred, he was somehow responsible, for the betrayal of his father to Khomeini's 'death squads' many years ago! They felt justice was best served by the Iranian, who had suffered as a result of his actions. Two British agents would make contact in the coming days, to furnish him with details and anything else he might require. It was enough of a lure for him; details were useful but equipment however, was vital! Only actions counted now! He handed his forged Iraqi passport to the Immigration officer and smiled. With luck, he'd be downing a nice cool drink, whilst watching bikini clad beauties at the hotel pool within the hour. He took religion the same way as his Tequila, with a pinch of salt, it had its uses but not on this mission.

The immigration officer handed the passport back and tapped the keyboard in front of him 'Albazi Hashimi; Iraqi carpet salesman' was now 'persona de interés' to the 'Grupo Especial de Operaciones (GEO)' anti-terrorist unit.

***

Day 12 … Sunday 8th May 2016

The voice of Reason

Rough hands shook Lamb awake 'Come on sleepy head you've got some explaining to do! Frankie's on the back terrace waiting, get yourself showered and changed and meet us out there in twenty minutes. I've put a mug of sweet black coffee on the dresser, it'll do you good' Billy winked then turned and left the room.

Lamb took a sip and almost burned his partially swollen lips. The inclusion of the unmentioned Brandy was appreciated. He checked his watch and was surprised to see it was almost noon, he'd slept soundly for around fourteen hours. After sorting himself out, he joined the others on the terrace.

Before he could speak Frankie held up his hand, a serious expression on his face, Lamb could sense the tension in the air. 'Tommy's been found, so I want you to quickly tell us what happened to him. Then go inside and have a word with Betty' seeing the questioning look on Lambs face he explained 'Its ok she knows all about you'

Lamb told them briefly how Jaycee had pushed Tommy to his death and how he'd set up a small barricade to stop the Jeep. He'd heard an explosion but Blue eyes one of the shirts had been unharmed because he'd shot at him. That was all he knew really, once he'd got back to the villa, he remembered nothing.

'Ok Lamb, tell Betty about Tommy and anything else she wants to know. If you can, try to underplay the part about the guns, she hates the bloody things. By the way, we've got something to tell you later' He pointed to the villa 'Now off you go, she's in the kitchen making you a full English, reckoned you'd be hungry … oh and ask her to send out more of that black coffee'

He made his way into the large kitchen and sat at the marble topped breakfast bar, already set for his meal.

'Good morning Mr Lamb or should I say good afternoon, my husband wanted to wake you earlier but I forbade it' she smiled 'He isn't very patient sometimes'. She placed his meal before him then sat on a stool opposite, studying him intently, her expression was now serious. 'Please go ahead, you must be starving'. When she saw that he'd relaxed a little and begun to eat she continued; 'Now first off, tell me exactly what happened to Tommy, leaving nothing out. Then I want to hear your story, from why you came here, right up to the present minute, more coffee?'

She listened politely, letting him tell it his way, she could see he found somethings difficult and she detected his anger when mentioning his wife and Sergio. Finally, when he'd finished, she waited a moment to let the emotions drain from him, sensing a release.

'Thank you, Martin, I can see that was difficult for you but you've answered my questions'. She smiled putting him at his ease 'You see, I had to be sure of your motives and why you involved my husband' she poured him another coffee. 'Now I can clearly tell that you are a decent man, trapped by terrible circumstances' she looked out to the terrace and Frankie showing a vulnerability that wasn't there a second ago. 'Tommy Jarvis died because a government killed him, not because you came here, the same goes for your friend' she searched his eyes 'You have an anger that most people would just accept, but not me, and neither would your wife!' He started to speak but she held up her hand 'No let me finish, then I must go to Tommy's wife Margaret and explain to her where the blame lies' she looked directly at him 'I assume you know of my illness' he nodded 'Yes, I would have liked to go to England but wherever I am with my husband, that is where I'm happiest. It's going to be very difficult for him in the coming months, but I want him to fight. Not for me Martin, and not just because what they are doing is wrong. They despise people like my husband, because he's not afraid to speak out, about the fact they are committing far greater evils. No ... I want him to fight to regain his pride' she paused her cheeks flushed 'I'm glad you're here' she touched his arm 'He's felt humiliated after the way they've treated him, and ok, he was a rogue, but he paid his dues and I want to think that when I'm gone he'll be the proud man he used to be' she held his hand 'The same as Mary your wife would have wanted for you' she rose and started to leave 'Please don't tell him all that I said' she paused at the doorway and turned to give him a mischievous smile 'We understand each other ... don't we Martin'

He returned to the terrace where Frankie and Billy were deep in conversation, no-one was smiling. 'You survived the grilling then eh Lamby, sit down we've got things to tell you and things to ask. First off Billy, we need a gin and tonic I reckon.' Frankie then told him of the events that had happened whilst he'd been missing and asleep. How a cyclist had since found Tommy at the bottom of a ravine, how they'd heard reports of a vehicle going off the track some miles further up in the hills and how the driver had died. At this point in time, the police appeared to be treating both as unrelated tragic accidents.

Lamb then explained in more detail everything that had happened to him and how the Americans were now involved. He also outlined his plans for their next move and what he required.

When he'd finished, Frankie walked to the balustrade that looked out on to the hillside, he stared out towards the mountains for what seemed a long while, then turned towards his companions with an expression Lamb hadn't seen before. 'Billy I want you to get hold of a few specialists, you know the sort, the one's Lamb here described' he turned to Lamb 'No more pussy footing around Lamb, if they want a fight they've got it, and yes I know they'll see these guys coming and going but that's what I want. They've got to realize we aren't gonna be intimidated' he looked over towards the hills again, holding a thought. 'Years ago I'd have trodden these insects into the dirt at the first sign of a threat, and that's the real reason Tommy's dead, not because of you, it's because I didn't react, I didn't protect him!' he walked over to Lamb and put his arm over his shoulder. 'We've got to come up with a plan for dealing with these bastards and I don't just mean the foot soldiers, I want the top, the ones who are controlling this, so get your thinking cap on'

Lamb looked at this new Frankie and saw in his mind's eye the hard villain of yesteryear. 'You asked when we would tell them that you know all about Bikini, well seems now is as good a time as any. Oh they'll have guessed already but it'll still take them off guard, they'll be wondering why tell us now?' he lowered his voice 'It'll scare the hell out of those at the top, whilst making those at the bottom feel as though they have to perform and do something about it quickly' he paused 'And by rushing it there's a good chance they'll make mistakes'

Frankie smiled 'Wish we'd have known each other years ago Lamby we'd have made a good team me and you' he laughed 'Once you'd been sorted out of course' he and Billy laughed together.

'Of course,' laughed Lamb quieter whilst running his tongue over the still loose tooth

'Good' said Frankie slapping Lamb on the back 'Now let's have a couple of drinks for Tommy, it'll dull the pain for a while, God only knows what's around the corner!'

Not just God … Fate knew too!

***

Sweat was forming on Mr Churchill's forehead and his breathing was coming in short gasps. 'Pontin please tell me this is a cruel hoax' he knew the answer before it came but his mind was racing 'How in hell could it have gotten so out of control. You told me this Lamb fellow was just an ignorant northerner, of no consequence to anyone' He had to force the next line 'Now you tell me he's killed an American? Are you seriously expecting me to believe that with all the resources at your disposal, neither you, nor the Yanks could contain the situation?' He listened to the reply '*They*' underestimated him?' he fumed, his voice tightening '*They*? You all underestimated him for Christ's sake!' he paused again 'Finish it! I don't care how, just do! A thought occurred to him 'Have you met up with the new asset yet, so we can draw back from this?' He listened 'Well, get onto it, make absolutely sure there's no way of tracing it back to us! And Pontin don't foul that up!' he slammed the phone down and slumped into the chesterfield. He noticed for the first time, that he could feel his heart beating and a cold shudder wracked his body 'Oh Christ!'

Fate sniggered!

***

      Albazi Hashimi cursed and turned his mobile off. His British contacts were on their way and he'd had to get rid of the stupid naive German girl he'd picked up the night before! Still there'd be other nights and other girls. After showering, he dressed in a yellow Lacoste t-shirt and grey slacks over which he wore a smart beige casual jacket. then made his way down to the reception of the AC Hotel Palicio,

Malaga. He chose a spot away from the entrance and partially hidden behind a marble column; it was a habit born from many years of the need to survive. They were unmistakable when they arrived, glancing around trying to look like casual observers. Both males, one with distinctive blue eyes and the second older, whom he gauged to be the more senior of the two, both wore similar shirts and sunglasses. He didn't approach them, why should he? They hadn't fooled him, he was involved just to do their dirty work! They must have their own motives but if the 'English man' had betrayed his father, what did it matter! However, he wouldn't faun to them, use them yes, that was different.

Spotting him, they approached, he didn't rise, the older one spoke first offering his hand 'Mr Hashimi?'

He ignored the gesture 'Possibly and you are?'

Warling paused deliberately 'Our names are immaterial, what is important is our information and the gift we bring, shall we retire to somewhere more discreet'

They walked out of the hotel and made their way down to a restaurant two blocks away. Once there, Warling and Hashimi found a booth at the back of the main bar. Wojtek split from the other two and found a table near the front window, from where he could observe the people in the street. Warling produced the plainly wrapped package he'd been carrying and pushed it towards his table companion 'A birthday pressent, I'm certain you'll find everything in there that you wished for'

Hashimi took the package and placed it out of sight on the seat beside him, he knew what it contained. Before agreeing to come to Spain he'd made certain demands, one of which was a Russian made PSS-2 silent pistol. It was manufactured by the secretive weapons developer, with the impossible to pronounce name 'TsNITochMash'. Mainly built for 'Spetsnaz' the state's special forces, he'd also asked for 24 rounds of its unique ammunition. The shell case of the bullet re-absorbed the noise creating explosive discharge, eliminating the need for a clumsy silencer. It had been his weapon of choice back in Iraq.

'You'll know where the Englishman is I trust, also can you give me his routine each day?'

Warling stared at the Iranian, he'd already decided they wouldn't get on, so there was no point in being polite 'Yes we know where he is but there is no routine, he's too clever for that' his tone had been sarcastic. He paused gauging the other man's reaction 'There are options; one of which would involve you going in to get him, whilst the other would be to just keep watch until he comes out'. He glanced around the bar to make sure they weren't being overheard 'Both of those options are unrealistic because of the villa's design and location' he leaned forward

'However I think we can draw him out' he gave a smug smile 'Inadvertently we may have already pre-arranged it' he looked at Hashimi who's puzzled expression had now changed to an impatient glare!

He laughed 'There's going to be a funeral … or even two' … he laughed again.

Fate summoned the Grim Reaper !

***

Day 13 ... Monday 9ᵗʰ May 2016

A Building Plot

     Lamb awoke feeling tired, he hadn't slept particularly well, it could have been the result of all the sleep he'd had the night before but somehow, he doubted that. No there was a new level of tension in the air, things were building up. In his own way he relished the fight but he was also aware of his limitations and the responsibility he had towards his new found allies. After showering and dressing, he made a decision on what he'd been pondering over for the last twenty-four hours. Then using the new mobile Frankie had bought him, he googled some information. Satisfied he made his way onto the rear terrace. Betty had set the side table with all the ingredients required for a full English; Wall's pork sausages, Sainsbury's premium bacon and Bury' black pudding, together with Heinz baked beans and Napoli whole tinned tomatoes. All this was complemented by the addition of Buttered white bread toast and Golden Shred marmalade. On the side; a pot of fresh Douwe Egbert's coffee gently simmered next to a bottle of Brandy de Jarez; this was after all, a grown-up breakfast.

He'd just made himself a bacon and sausage sandwich when he heard footsteps approaching.

'Morning Lamb' it was Billy and he had a sheet of paper in his hand 'I've got a list of those items you asked for if you want to check it. They've all arrived and I've had them taken to the locations and hidden as you wanted. Don't worry, the only people who'll find them will be us'

'Thanks Billy, by the way do you still have the phone you used to call the number in the newspaper, the one accusing me of being a fraudster?'

'Yes mate, do you want it?'

'Not now but I will later if you answer yes to the next question'

'Go on I'm listening'

'Ok I'm after a real con-merchant, well con-woman actually; it involves quite a bit of deception over the course of a couple of days. Do you know of one who might help?'

Billy grinned 'Got someone in mind already, name of Jocelyne Bell, she could sell choirs to the Welsh. She's in the UK but I know she'll jump at the chance, no questions asked, absolutely loves Frankie and Betty. I'll give her a call now and get her out here tomorrow, anything special I should tell her'

'Just put her on standby for now Billy, tell her she'll be using her own name and that from now on she's a freelance reporter, and tell her you'll be in touch within the next couple of days'.

'Will do' Billy looked down at his list 'I've also got two Scottish guys on standby. Lord or Laird Caithstead, not a real Lord by the way and his partner Ghille Jock, not a real Ghille neither. Caithstead was Jock's commanding officer in the British army many years ago, crack shots the pair of them. They used to charge punters a fortune to go up to Scotland Grouse shooting. Only thing is, the Grouse didn't belong to them. Whilst they'd pretend to be driving the birds towards the guns, they'd actually be driving back down the M6. They'd leave the punters to explain themselves to the police and the real Laird, characters the pair of them'

'They sound ideal Billy; reassure them they won't actually be shooting anyone' and the other stuff?'

'Yes, sorted, all fifty thousand euros worth, it's somewhere safe ready to be put in its place as you asked'

'One last task Billy, I'll need a jiffy bag and I'd like the thirty-eight thousand euros cash, placed inside it, along with a faint trace of the drugs. Hang on to that map we used to find the goatherd's finca as well' he looked out across the valley 'I've just got to find a way to deal with the American or Americans if they send others'

Billy started to walk away when Lamb called after him 'Hold on a second mate, any chance we can find out where all those bastards are staying?'

'No problem I've already put word out; it shouldn't take long'

'Thanks Billy, by the way next time you're out and about, gently start a rumour that some strangers are trying to offload a large number of drugs in the area, it could be a useful to us'

Ten minutes later Frankie appeared

'Morning Frankie I've just been speaking to Billy, so once you've had breakfast, I'll bring you up to speed'. He paused gauging Frankie's mood 'I'd like to know what arrangements have been made for Tommy's funeral and whether or not I should attend. I feel guilty as hell about what happened to him'

Frankie frowned and when he spoke it was with a vulnerability Lamb hadn't seen before. 'Tommy was a good man and a loyal friend' he paused, good memories fighting with the raw sorrow of the moment 'We worked together many times over the years. Even knowing what might happen, he'd have still done the same, so bin the guilt okay Lamby' he gripped his new friend's shoulders 'I mean it! I knew him and you feeling guilty was the last thing he'd want!' he looked out towards the hills.

'The guilt lies with the evil swine out there and he'll be resting easy in the knowledge the one who killed him, died up there too' he shook Lamb slightly to emphasise the words 'That's thanks to you, and I know he'd have appreciated it' he released his grip. 'As for the funeral, Margaret's taking him back to Blighty. They're going to give him a proper east end send-off' he looked towards the house 'I can't go, I checked, the bastards, won't even let me in for that … Betty will be there though' his voice choked on the edge of breaking. 'Lamb when all this is sorted and we get back there, we'll both visit him eh!' he shook his head to clear the dark thoughts still haunting him 'Anyway, what's our next move Lamby? I don't do inaction too well, not once I've set my mind to it and trust me its action I want now'

Lamb turned to lean on the balustrade and thought of their next move. He had a plan and sensed events were coming to a head, four men had died already and Frankie was angry and impatient for movement.

'I'm going to make a call first Frankie, see if we can't drive a wedge in their ranks, I'll pass on our ultimatum at the same time. I will tell it straight though, if we tried to bluff, they'd cotton on immediately'

He pulled out his mobile and dialled'

'Pontin speaking, I've been expecting you Mr Lamb, I hear you've now included murder to your list of misdemeanours, it really is getting out of hand'

Lamb cut through him 'Still in there with your stupid remarks eh Pontin, hardly my fault if the stupid yank took off-roading to a new depth' he paused confident that his attempt at humour was hitting home. 'We're both aware it doesn't matter if you trace this call, you already know where I am. Listen carefully though' he took a deep breath 'As you'll already have guessed, I'm not the only person aware of the facts behind operation Bikini., there's someone else. The reason I'm confirming that, is because your American partners killed a friend of his, an innocent man' Pontin tried to interrupt but Lamb cut across him 'Don't treat me as a fool ok! What they did changed everything, far from intimidating him they escalated the situation' he now paused to let Pontin have his rant.

'That was just the Americans, we had no part of it. If anyone is to blame though, it's you for involving that mobster you call your friend, also by killing their agent, you've made them very angry!'

Lamb now cut him short again 'Here's how it stands and this is the final ultimatum. You must listen to what I'm saying and I'll make it very clear for you.

I don't want your men recalled, I have my own plans for them, they aren't going anywhere'

'Got a taste for murder now have we Lamb, because if …'

Lamb stopped him 'I won't waste my breath arguing, it's way past that stage and the same applies to the American Harkant' he let his remarks sink in. 'Firstly, my friend the mobster 'as you call him' and his wife are to be granted permission to return to the UK, with no interference from the government. Secondly, I will resume my life as I see fit' he paused again 'Now as I see it, that's not a lot to ask!'

'I don't think you're in a position to dictate terms Lamb. What assurances do we get that this so-called Bikini Project' you keep mentioning, will remain a secret? Bearing in mind, the government, if it was involved and I'm certainly not suggesting it is, would never agree to blackmail!'

Lamb let out a sardonic laugh 'Now you're taking the piss, you approve murder but claim to have ethics' he shook his head in disbelief. 'You already know, I'm reluctant to reveal the facts behind Bikini, because of the seriousness of the consequences. However, you stupidly decided to start killing and now you've pushed it too far to go back. Because of that decision, my associate has no such compulsions. Also, if anything happens to him, trust me, I will blow this thing into the open without a second thought!' he spoke slowly but firmly 'But I believe, even at this stage, it can still be contained at a local level. However, that is only if you agree to do exactly as I ask!'

Pontin protested 'This is ridiculous; we the British have not killed anyone! If, and that's only if' ... a decision was made to kill, it certainly wouldn't be mine. From what I've heard, you're the only one who's killed someone. So, even if I did agree to your terms, the Americans would never sign up to it. They're pissed off and they'll still see it as blackmail ... no, they want their pound of flesh and that means you being silenced, their way!' he let it sink in. 'However, it doesn't have to be that way, we can protect you, so you still have time to sort this out in a sensible manner' he paused. 'Just meet us in a place of your choosing and let us discuss it as grown men, we can discuss the yanks then'

Lamb shut him up 'The Americans need sorting out today Pontin, they're your problem, or should I say your boss's. With my deal, it's all parties or none and don't confuse blackmail with insurance!' he spoke slowly. 'In our situation, it's a one-off payment, in the form of an agreement. The incriminating evidence will be buried for the duration, with safeguards on both sides. That way, so long as we protect each other's interests, it will stay at status quo. The way the world's going, it'll eventually become irrelevant anyway'

'How can we be sure it will stay that way? Your gangster friend's past isn't exactly reassuring'

'And yours is I suppose?' he laughed 'Unbelievable! don't act the innocent, or that you haven't got a choice, I've just given you one. You owe nothing to these poncey clowns on the ground, give them up and get this sorted! I'm sure that's what your boss wants, he must be crapping himself right now!' He paused, listening to the rapid breathing coming from the man he was talking to, his bullets were obviously hitting home. 'That's it Pontin, it's that simple! However and pay real attention to this; if just one more innocent person gets hurt, I'll take that as a definite rejection' he waited, but no reply came 'I'll be in touch'

'Wait! there's something you need to know'

Lamb froze, there was a new urgency in Pontin's voice

'Go on Pontin, what is it?'

'That bar owner friend of yours, the one who's death you're wrongly blaming us for'

'Go ahead, I'm still listening'

'He had a daughter living in Malaga, name of Carmen, mother of two kids. Well she's in Nerja, staying in her father's restaurant. He's already been buried but she's been arranging the remembrance service for Saturday the 14th. It's been delayed, until his sick mum is well enough to fly over from Columbia'

'So you've got other people on the ground eh? It's very interesting that you'd pour resources into something you deny knowledge of. Anyway, I already knew about the service and why its delayed, so why are you telling me about the daughter Pontin, why the concern? She's nothing to do with our business!'

'Our resources as you call them, are just local newspaper reports, we only monitored them because you drew the area to our attention'

Lamb scoffed 'You're so full of it Pontin, but go on'

'Well, we wouldn't want anything to happen to her, would we? you might think badly of us, especially with what you just mentioned in your terms'

Lamb was furious 'Is that a veiled threat Pontin? That's a new low even for you. You know damn well if anything happened to her, the subsequent enquiry by the Spanish, would blow this whole thing open, or … 'he stopped suddenly, as an alarm went off in his brain 'Wait! … are you trying to tell me someone else is involved in all of this … apart from you and the yanks?' he paused again 'And you're worried, they may harm her?'

'That's not what I said … but' he deliberately didn't finish the sentence.

'Who is it? … why would they hurt her and why can't you stop them?'

'Insurance I think you called it Lamb, someone took out insurance' he hung up.

Hashimi frowned, other than flying he disliked travelling by public transport, even if it was a taxi, it made him feel vulnerable. In Iraq, he'd owned a matt black range rover, armoured and with blacked out windows. The mere sight of it terrified those he hunted, like the grim reaper, it came only to collect their souls. Now he was on his way to Nerja, the two Englishmen had assured him his target would turn up there *'almost one hundred percent guaranteed, either the 13th or 14th'* the older one had said.

No rush, they were paying him handsomely, however, that was a mere bonus compared to avenging his family's honour. In the meantime, he'd relax in a comfortable hotel and get to know the area … and the women of course. They'd booked him into the luxurious Parador Hotel, it was close to Quixote's and the bait. He gave a wry smile at the thought that had just come to mind, he was now on his own. There were no contingencies for his recall, he would do whatever it took to get his target, including taking out any so-called innocents that might get in his way.

There was no such thing as collateral damage in his world!

***

Day 14 … Tuesday 10th May 2016

Reach for the Star

Edward Warling followed Filip Wojtek down the marble stairs to the hotel reception, where they both checked out. They were following protocol by not staying in the same hotel for more than three days. The reason for doing this was quite simple; If, after switching hotels, the same faces were seen in close proximity to the new locations, it would be more than a coincidence. It would thus expose those who were tracking or watching them. They weren't going far, just to the smart Hotel San Cristobal further down the harbour front, it wasn't necessary to go miles away.

However, it was a protocol that would ultimately come back to haunt them!

They'd been busy during the past couple of days; making arrangements for the arrogant Iranian, whilst drawing up plans to draw Lamb and his gangster friend out of their citadel. Lamb had been easy to sort; he wouldn't be able to resist retuning to Nerja for his friend's funeral service … and into the path of the waiting assassin.

Francis Lane on the other hand, was a different kettle of fish; they'd need to target someone close to him to draw him out. He hadn't responded to the death of his colleague Tommy, not yet anyway. However, if another of his party were to get into trouble, they were absolutely certain he wouldn't be able to contain himself. His anger and loyalty to those around him were his weak points. They'd need to act swiftly and decisively, before he had a chance to release whatever knowledge of Bikini' he might have!

The Shirts had taken it in turns with Harkant, to monitor the activities up at Frankie Lane's villa. They'd been able see the road leading to his front gate, through binoculars whilst hidden in the tree line up in the hills. It hadn't taken too long to establish a pattern, after all that was their job, now they just needed to put a plan into action.

Whilst observing the villa, one routine had stood out during Lane's attempts to secure his home. Each evening, one of his men, wearing a red baseball cap, would come out through the gates and walk a large German Shepherd dog around the perimeter, Warling figured there must be a way to exploit this but currently he wasn't sure how. The priority was to separate Lamb and the gangster, but even then, they'd need to kill them at exactly the same time. Neither, must be given the opportunity to release their information in revenge for the other's death.

Wojtek looked at his companion and smiled, he sensed it wouldn't be long before his specialist skills were required.

***

Although he'd had an early night, Lamb had endured a restless sleep, the words of Pontin still echoing in his mind;

'Well we wouldn't want anything to happen to her, would we? or you might think badly of us'

He'd already guessed there would be a trap waiting for him in Nerja. Pontin's actions puzzled him, why tell him they knew about the funeral service? It just didn't make sense! He'd been wrestling with it all night. Pontin had even hinted that someone other than the shirts and the Americans were involved, why? If they were going to ambush him, it would be stupid to warn him like that!

In the early hours whilst not being able to sleep, he'd googled an address, … there it was, the one he'd hoped for. He wouldn't let the others know about it, not yet anyway. What he was hoping for, might not even happen and he didn't want to get their hopes up. He showered, dressed and made his way out to the rear terrace.

After everyone had sorted out their caffeine, nicotine and in some cases alcohol levels, Lamb guided Frankie and Billy out towards the edge of the terrace. He told them of Pontin's message and the inference that a third party might be threatening Sergio's family.

He explained further 'The Shirts and the Americans wouldn't dare touch them, as the Spanish police would link that to Sergio's death and investigate. However, that wouldn't be a concern to a complete stranger, brought in from somewhere else and not previously involved!'

'Billy voiced everyone's thoughts 'So who else would be involved in this, considering it's so top secret?'

Frankie added his thoughts 'Yes good point Billy, they can't just ask any old hitman to join in, they'd be subjecting themselves to the type of exposure they're now trying to avoid!'

Lamb gasped 'I'm so stupid! it's so bloody obvious, I can't believe it!' he looked at them, waiting for a response 'There were three parties involved in the Bikini Project ... UK, USA and ...' he stopped as the realisation hit his friends.

Frankie said it for all of them 'Iraq!'

Lamb built on the theory 'Yes, it would be the only people they could trust. If that's what they've done. It shouldn't be too hard to spot anyone from that part of the world, watching the bar and waiting for me to turn up!' … He took a deep breath … 'Hold on a minute though' the others stared at him 'There's another reason why Pontin warned me, it's just occurred to me … and it's so obvious … They want me to go to Nerja! … If I do go after this other person, they'll know exactly where I am! … They don't care what happens to the Iraqi, if that's what he is … he's just the bait! It would mean they could keep an eye on me, whilst they dealt with you Frankie … Then, it would be my turn! … The crafty bastards!' He could see the others understood.

Lamb realised at that moment, they would need serious help in identifying and neutralizing the killer, or killers: That were now being rallied against them! The war was to be fought on two fronts and pretty soon innocent people would start dying! He couldn't allow that! Frankie's soldiers were not naturally violent. Yes, they did act without question through an unspoken code of loyalty. With them it was 'threaten one threaten all' but they never randomly killed! … It just wasn't their way! … Back in their old days, it was a good thumping or kicking and only then in retaliation'

Lamb recognised what they might not, … that in today's dangerous world 'hurt' had been replaced by 'kill' and 'respect' by 'fear'. It was a cruel fact and it stalked anyone and everywhere!

Billy broke into his thoughts 'I've a few friends in Nerja, I'll ask them to keep an eye out for any obvious strangers'.

'Thanks Billy, and see if they can get a photo asap, I've a hunch it could be important' he frowned, then made a decision 'Give me a minute gents' he removed the phone from his shirt pocket, then crossed the terrace to the villa to take advantage of the shade. He typed in the address he'd googled earlier, then added a short message;

'M1003 (MGM-31C) - (SS-1d) Modification Requirements' (36.785- 3.804)

He pressed send, absolutely certain that 3,500 miles away, this would grab someone's attention!

He returned to his, by now, curious friends and before they could speak, asked 'Frankie are we still walking the dog in the evenings as we discussed?'

'Yes, near enough the same time each day, we vary it slightly so as not to make it too obvious'

'Good, is he still wearing the red baseball cap? It's an important detail' he looked past Frankie's puzzled expression 'Ok both, as you know I've been referring to a plan' they nodded 'Well recent events suggest the Shirts and the Yank aim to hit us on the 14th, the day of Sergio's remembrance service. So, I reckon we now take control of this and bring our own plan forward to the 13th'

Frankie looked across at Billy 'What do you reckon, can you sort everything by then?'

Billy nodded in confirmation.

Lamb stood up and raised his glass 'Here's to Friday the 13th ... unlucky for some' he looked across at the villa with serious concern and sat down 'Alright Frankie, I guess you'll need to tell Betty eh?'

Frankie turned to face the same direction 'She won't be back from Tommy's funeral until Thursday evening and I reckon she'd rather not know mate. But she will have guessed something is happening, she always could'

Lamb walked over to the balustrade and paused. He'd been mulling over an idea and the time seemed right to put it into play straight away. He walked back to his companions 'Billy, remember I asked you if you still had the phone you used, to call that dodgy Serious Overseas Fraud Office number?'

'Yes, I do, it's in my room, I haven't used it since, wasn't sure if I should' he frowned 'Do you want it now?'

'Yes, but not for me mate, I want you to contact our lady reporter' he explained what he wanted Billy to say 'Afterwards could you grab us some G and T's, we need to get this plan clear in our heads and it could take a while 'Frankie shall we retire to your concrete block?'

'Cheeky sod! It's marble dining furniture' he laughed 'Oi Billy, cheap crap Gin for the scouse git, bleedin concrete indeed'

When Billy returned, Lamb explained his plan. It was complex, audacious and risky but with the right actors, it just might work.

An important part of the plan involved Frankie doing two things;

- o First, he'd need to present himself at the local 'Guardia Civil' headquarters.
- o Secondly, he'd have to make two vital phone calls.

If either of these didn't happen, then the whole plan collapsed, timing was imperative!

The next two days were spent finalising the details of the plan; making phone calls, rallying the troops and repeatedly going over the details. They needed to decide on options, in the event of the inevitable glitches.

He knew from his army days, plans rarely survive the first hour but so long as alternatives are pre-prepared, they do have a chance of success.

***

Warling took the call from Pontin and turned to his companion 'Filip, call Harkant and ask him to meet us in the Blue Surf bar down the road, shall we say in half an hour? There's been an interesting development'

A short while later, once everyone was settled with a drink, Warling explained the details of the message he'd received from Pontin.

'There's been a communication between someone up at the villa and a reporter in London. We know it's from the villa as they used the same phone as before. It could be they are planning to release some or all of the information they hold' he stopped to let the significance of his words sink in 'Obviously this cannot be allowed!'

Wojtek cursed 'I knew we should have just gone in there and wiped the lot out'

'Yes Filip, I know that's what you'd have liked, but we are supposed to do this without drawing attention to ourselves. A massacre would hardly achieve that, would it? I'm sure our American friend here would agree with me'

Lynden Harkant studied the younger of the two men. He confirmed to himself the belief, that whilst most Limeys were oddballs, this one was a special case 'Yeah I'd agree with that'

Warling continued 'I'm still confident we can entice Lamb go to the funeral service, … and when he does, there's no doubt our middle eastern comrade, will take care of him. There'll be no clues to trace it back to us; the Spanish authorities will assume it's a terrorist or revenge killing. If Hashimi does get caught, that's just bad luck on his part. He knows nothing of who we really are, or our involvement' he smiled at his fellow conspirators 'Hopefully though, he'll do us the favour of dying as a martyr in a shootout! We are pretty certain his passport is forged and I am reliably informed that if requested, our own agencies, through subtle means of course, will assist the Spanish to confirm it as such'

Harkant joined in, he wasn't going to let the Brit assume command over him, he had his own agenda. 'I have a personal interest in Lamb's death remember?' He stopped to make sure he'd got their attention. 'And I haven't met this Hashimi guy, we only have your people's word that he's any good' the jibe wasn't lost on Warling 'So as I'm intending to go there, I'll need to know what he looks like'

'A correct decision Lynden, however, just remember, the whole point of Hashimi being there, is mainly to draw Lamb out and to divert attention away from us'

Secretly, Wojtek was enjoying the battle of wills between the two older men. Warling's condescending manner towards the American added to his amusement. He also wanted to see Lamb die, though if he couldn't do it himself, then the knowledge of his certain death would have to suffice.

There were other victims nearer to hand who would satisfy his blood lust.

Warling continued 'You will do what you must Lynden, it may well be better that way. We, by that I mean, Filip and I, will concentrate on this reporter woman. She can't be allowed to find out anything. Hopefully, we can intercept her, or at least find out where she'll be meeting the gangster and his friend' he mused for a moment 'It's doubtful that they'd take her back to the villa. After all, they don't know we are aware of her imminent arrival' he was thinking it through 'And the last thing they will want, is for us to find out that they're about to reveal '*The secret*'. He faced his blue-eyed companion 'So Filip, why don't you ask our office to let us know more about her? Especially when she's due to arrive, we can then meet and track her'

***

Sitting at his polished Burr Walnut desk, with its red Moroccan leather inlay and ornate brass handles. Mr Churchill swivelled in his green, buttoned, Chesterfield office chair and stared out of the window. He was transfixed by the vapour trails of an unseen aircraft, as it made its way to some far-off destination. His mind carried him into the first-class cabin and thoughts of Champagne, Caviar and exotic destinations, merely added torture to his already troubled mind.

He was shaken out of his reverie by the red phone ringing on the desk in front of him.

He answered it reluctantly 'Mr Lincoln, you surprised me calling today, I thought you'd be pre-occupied with the senate vote on your budg …' He stopped, cut off by the angry rant in his ear and waited for it to subside. 'There really is no need for the tone you are adopting, as from what I've been told, everything is now being sorted'. He raised his eyes to look up at the vapour trails again, but like his dreams they had evaporated. 'Oh God' he muttered, more to himself than the phone. 'No Mr Lincoln, I wasn't addressing you, it was someone slightly higher'
He let the other man start to explain himself, then frustratingly, cut in. 'Mr Lincoln it seems we are both getting conflicting reports from our agents, this needs to be sorted immediately' he listened again whilst a cold shudder went down his spine 'I know nothing of any contact with a reporter, are you sure?' He sat bolt upright, the first traces of sweat forming on his brow.

'Well of course this changes everything, but we can no longer deal with this by merely physical means' he stopped, as a question was fired at him. 'Mr Lincoln, by that I meant there are certain limits, beyond which our actions alone, could betray the secret we are trying to hide!' he let the other man absorb the observation

'Well yes that is a consideration, however the gangster as you call him is being portrayed here in the UK as a serious drug dealer, it would look very odd if we just let him return. And if we did find a way, would he betray his new friend?'

He listened to the American 'Well yes, thinking about it that way he possibly might for the sake of his dying wife!' the voice at the other end spoke animatedly as he waited. 'Well, you will have noticed that I didn't say 'we' would have to honour any deal once she's died' the other man continued 'Yes of course, I agree we can never do a deal with Lamb, it's gone way too far for that, his days are numbered anyway!

'Yes, Mr Lincoln you have a nice day too'

He picked up his secure phone and dialled a number, his face red with rage, 'Pontin you'd better have a bloody good explanation for not telling me about this dammed reporter woman!' he listened to the reply 'Oh so you were going to tell me later were you?' He lowered his voice trying but failing to take the anger out of it 'What do you mean you were waiting to confirm it? It's just been confirmed to me by the dammed Americans!' He took a deep breath 'Well in future I want to be the first to know! I do not want to find out what's going on over there, from some bloody yank! Wait there!' he put the phone down and walked to the window to get a grip of his foul mood.

The first drops of the impending storm spattered on the glass 'Bloody typical'

He returned to the phone and remained standing as Pontin relayed the message from Lamb 'How can we be sure he's telling the truth about terms, and ask yourself, if he is genuine why does he need a reporter?' He cut the reply off 'Let me make this clear, there will be no deal with him! The gangster on the other hand ...' he let the sentence tail off there was no need to finish it.

When the call ended, he crossed the room to look at a large gilt framed picture. It was changed regularly and this one was on loan from the Royal Academy. Oil on canvas, it was by the American artist Benjamin West. He leaned forward to read the ornately engraved words on the small brass plaque at the bottom 'Oliver Cromwell Dissolving the Long Parliament' his shoulders slumped 'Oh my God is everyone taking the piss'

Fate was doing irony

***

Day 16 … Thursday 12ᵗʰ May 2016

Once upon a time!

It was mid-morning as Jocelyne Bell walked through the arrival's hall at Malaga airport. She saw the man holding up a sign with her name on it and smiled. He took her case and beckoned her to follow.

'Jocie' Bell, 50 years old, with flowing red hair and the figure of a much younger woman, had jumped at the chance to help Frankie and Betty. Following a disruptive childhood, thanks mainly to an alcoholic mother and an absent father, she'd gotten out of control and spent various terms in remand homes. It was during this period that she'd locked horns with Frankie and his mob. Instead of punishing her, he'd seen a spark of his old self and had persuaded Betty to take her under her wing. Whilst still a smooth-talking fraudster, she now had respect, both for herself and the wealthy clients' she targeted.

She'd come to Spain at the request of a friend. After the initial contact, Billy had e-mailed a script over to her, explaining her cover story and the way he wanted her to play it during the forthcoming phone conversation with him.

It had gone like clockwork;

'Yes Mr Cooper, she was indeed a freelance reporter who specialised in the *exclusive exposé.* However, before she'd agree to even listen to what information he had, there were certain terms and conditions, that everyone involved, would need to comply with!

- First, for her own safety she always used a pseudonym when submitting a story. They must therefore promise' not to reveal her real name when the story broke.
- Second, they would also have to guarantee, that certain security arrangements were in place, as she was in the habit of making enemies.
- Third, they must ensure that no other persons beyond those immediately involved, would know her real identity or the reason for the meetings.
- Finally, any information given would have to be backed up by physical evidence! That was of vital importance, no proof and she wouldn't use it!'

All this was said, in the almost certain knowledge, that Billy Cooper's phone was being monitored, by the listening agencies at GCHQ and Fort Meade!'

She followed her greeter to the pristine white Mercedes A class sedan and climbed into the back seat. He opened the trunk and took her small silver suitcase to the rear of the vehicle. She knew him well, although until this moment, she hadn't been aware that 63-year-old Johnny 'The Chauffeur' Kinsel was also helping Frankie out, after Tommy's 'accident'

They were both experienced enough not to visually acknowledge each other.

As he was placing the luggage inside the boot, he covertly glanced around to scan the other vehicles, noting as many as he could. Three rows back, one stood out from the others; a black BMW X5 with darkened side windows, similar to the one that had been described to him.

Two men in white shirts and sunglasses were just climbing into it!

Following the '*salida*' exit signs, he turned to pass in front of the suspicious vehicle as it waited to pull out from its bay. On the driver's door, he could just discern the scratched letters 'YNWA' confirming it to be the Shirts' motor. Once on the AP-7 motorway, he only used his side mirrors to monitor the other vehicle's progress behind him. Experience had taught him long ago, that people in the vehicle following you, tended to notice you watching them if you constantly looked in the internal rear-view mirror.

The black 4 x 4 maintained its station, three hundred yards behind, until Johnny pulled off the motorway; then it closed the gap to just two cars lengths.

Forty-five minutes later, Jocie was dropped off at the very smart four-star Park Plaza Suites hotel, Puerto Banus, to refresh herself. An hour after that, she'd showered and changed into a sleeveless lemon top and white slacks. To complement the look, she was also carrying her favourite, white 'Bulgari' handbag, purchased during a recent trip to Harrods. She then made her way down to the high-class Belvedere restaurant, on the harbour front, for lunch and her first meeting. The contact' she had been told 'Would be sitting outside and wearing a red baseball cap' all subsequent arrangements would be made through him.

Retribution had just nudged fate aside!

***

Billy walked over and joined Lamb, sitting at the marble patio table. He was just having his third 'Americano' coffee of the morning. In this one, he'd also added a liberal measure of Torres 20-year-old Brandy, 'to adjust his levels!'

Billy smiled 'Got a couple of good results from Nerja Lamby. Not hundred percent positive it's our man … but we do have a photo of a foreign guy, like you asked us to look out for. I'll WhatsApp it across. … His behaviour seems to fit'

Both men went quiet, concentrating on their mobiles.

Billy continued 'He arrived Monday afternoon and has been sitting at the bar opposite Quixote's every day since, Definitely seems to be watching the daughter sorting her father's place out. Bit creepy too, he likes leering at the younger women. Personally, I reckon it is him, so how do you want us to deal with it?'

Lamb opened the picture 'I reckon I agree with you mate' he enlarged the image 'Do we know what time this was taken Billy?'

'Well I received it about an hour ago, so somewhere around nine this morning, why?'

'Well mate, judging by the shape of the glass he's holding and the colour of what's in it, that's a straight Brandy he's drinking. … With ice but there's no mixer on the table. Bit early in the day don't you reckon Billy?' the other man smiled, the words kettle and black springing to mind 'So, it seems our man likes to over indulge himself, with booze and women'

Billy said it for them both 'He's almost behaving like it's his first holiday in Spain'

'Exactly, and those clothes of his, they look bloody expensive' he enlarged the picture further 'He's also wearing what could be a Rolex Submariner watch … what's the betting that it's real!' he looked up 'No doubt about it, he's dressed to impress'. Both men fell silent, processing the information 'And I've a final thought Billy, if he does like a bit of action, why is he off the beaten track and not strutting his stuff down at Burriana beach?'

Any doubts they may have had, disappeared … they'd found their man.

'Alright Billy, as for dealing with him leave it to me. I don't want to say too much at this point, in case what I'm hoping for doesn't come off. I promise I'll explain later' his friend acknowledged him, so he continued 'Ok, you said a couple of results, what's the second?'

'Those shirt guys you described; they were at the airport watching for Jocie. Seems you were right about that too. Looks like the plan is working'

'Early days yet Billy, but just what I wanted to hear'. Lamb opened his e-mails, typed in the simple address, then attached the picture from his gallery and pressed send. If his hunch was right, there was a good chance the recipients would know the man, and if so, they'd be in touch within hours.

'You all set to meet with our reporter friend Billy?'

'Sure, it's all sorted, Johnny, who picked her up from the airport, has passed on the details. We're treating her on a need to know basis, only telling her what's relevant hour by hour. That way, it looks more natural and authentic to any outside observer. She's happy with that, born actress is our Jocie, she really knows how to wing it'

***

An operative, thousands of miles away, read an e-mail and alerted her supervisor. 'Matador' the code name they'd assigned to the sender, was drip feeding them more information. Within the hour, a specially trained agent using advanced technology and search techniques, had identified the man in the photograph. He was an Iranian, previously known to them under various aliases and also his real name 'Albazi Hashimi'. It was also confirmed, that knowledge of him dated back to pre-Gulf war days. Then, his actions against innocent Israelis, had made him an enemy of the state. All that, was after he'd moved to Iraq, as one of Saddam Hussain's top fixers.

That revelation, along with the previous cryptic information about the missiles, was sufficient justification to act. They were to put a large team together and dispatch it immediately to Spain. They'd identified the Nerja area, using the co-ordinates supplied in the first communication.

A coded reply was immediately sent to Matador. Now that the mission was on an official footing, all protocols would be strictly adhered to. Not only was their own secrecy vital, but it was equally important to protect the source. Once on the ground in Spain, they would first observe and then secure their immediate area.

After all, there was still the possibility of it being a terrorist trap.

A new highly motivated and experienced player had entered the game and they had deadly skills!

***

Billy stood up as Jocelyne Bell introduced herself, then adjusted the back of her wicker chair as she sat down.

She let out a faint laugh and smiled at him 'Thank you, there are still a few gentlemen left then?'

He smiled back 'Not really, it's pretty much the norm out here' then realising the implication of what he'd said 'But that doesn't mean I'm not a gentleman it's just …' he stopped as she held her hand up laughing.

'It's ok I get it' she looked straight into his eyes catching him off guard and adding to his awkwardness. Apart from Betty it had been a long time since he'd talked one to one with a woman.

The spell was broken by the arrival of the waiter. Billy smiled again 'Can I get you a drink er …' he hesitated 'I'm sorry, how would you like me to address you?'

'Well, if I can call you Billy, you may call me Jocie, and thank you I'll have a Tinto verano to start with, ice and a slice'

They'd actually known each other for many years and she'd always had a soft spot for Frankie's right-hand man, the tough guy with gentle ways. Now however, they were acting out their respective roles.

The curtains had gone up, the stage was set, Act one of the play had just begun!

***

Having followed their target, from the airport, via the hotel, to the bar. Warling and Wojtek, now wearing Ralph Lauren striped shirts and Chinos sat at a table just behind the female reporter and the man with the red baseball cap. Without showing an obvious interest, they strained to hear the dialogue between the couple. From what snippets they could hear, it seemed a meeting was definitely being arranged and hopefully they'd be able to follow her, whenever that happened.

Luck then provided the bait and cast them a line.

***

Billy spoke to his table companion in a hushed tone, whilst furtively glancing up at the street. 'The meeting will be tomorrow evening, at a remote place in the hills north of the town' he looked out across the road. 'I'm not going to say the location here, for obvious reasons, but it is secure' he paused, 'I don't want to say any exact times here either, but suffice to say tomorrow evening. Johnny will pick you up. Don't worry about him, he doesn't know why you're here, or what we're going to discuss. Anyway, the important details, times etcetera, are on the map I'm going to give you' he looked up at her gauging her reaction 'Any problems with what I've said so far?'

She shook her head 'Can't you give me any clue as to what it's about, not even a tiny cryptic one?'

He frowned 'Sorry, but trust me, when you do find out you'll realize why'

He reached into his pocket and looked up and down the street again, before partially unfolding a Michelin map on the table. Drawn on it in red crayon were a few short lines of writing and a small circle.

Above that, secured with a paper clip, was a passport sized photo of himself.

He shielded it with his right arm 'Because of the secrecy and to demonstrate to you that we can be trusted, I've had this map marked up with the location and times' he put his finger on the red circle and she raised her eyebrows enquiringly 'Yes I know it looks remote, but it is safe … and secure' he continued 'The general idea, is that you can have it placed in the hotel safe, with instructions to have it followed up, if you don't return by a certain time. Or you can do nothing. it's up to you, Anyway, it's your choice and along with my mugshot it's also your insurance' She started to speak but he stopped her 'It's ok we trust you already' he was cut off by her mobile phone ringing

She looked apologetically at him 'Sorry about this but it might be important' and pressed answer.

He waved his hand 'Not at all, you carry on, why don't I go and get us another drink … same as last time?'

She smiled and gave him the thumbs up, then mouthed the words 'Yes please' and returned her attention to the caller.

'Hello … yes, it is, who's that? … sorry I can't hear you very clearly … Mom is that you? Yes, I'm fine … what?' she placed a hand over her ear 'Look you'll have to speak up … no it's no good, hold on a second' she rose and moved out onto the pavement, then took two steps to the left but with her back to the table, just three feet away 'That's better … in Spain I told you … yes I did, yesterday … I said I was coming here to … no I definitely told you … ok … have it your way then, go on' she paused, feigning exasperation, whilst pretending to listen to a fictitious rant, about next door's cat and the soaring cost of margarine.

Johnny, sitting across the road with a mobile phone to his ear, marvelled at her acting skills.

***

Warling rose and took a step towards the item of interest on the nearby table. Holding his phone concealed in the palm of his right hand, he passed it smoothly over the map and took a serious of continuous shots. Then carrying on forward, he walked into the bar just as the woman's companion was coming out 'Beautiful day again' he said looking for, but not seeing, any sign of recognition.

***

Billy and Jocie ordered lunch; avocado salad for her and pizza diavola for him, washed down with a shared bottle of Gran Vina Sol and bottled still water.

The small talk gently carried them towards the mid-afternoon, with both people enjoying each other's company. Billy reassured her that someone would be watching over her, then made his excuses 'See you tomorrow then Jocie' he leaned closer, lowering his voice 'Take care of the map'

'Ok' she hesitated 'Maybe we could have a late dinner tomorrow evening, when it's all over?'

He smiled and reached out to touch her hand 'That would be nice Miss Bell, but for the rest of today and tomorrow, you should just relax and enjoy the beach, or whatever' his hand lingered on hers for a little while longer than would be normal 'And don't forget, you'll have a story to prepare'. A strange mixture of hollowness and excitement churned his insides 'Tomorrow then'. He turned as Johnny pulled the white Mercedes, into the kerb. Billy's night was far from over, he also had a meeting with some of the other cast members, he needed to be focused, lives depended on it!

Act one; the meeting' was over, Act two; the reckoning' was about to begin.

***

Earlier, Johnny had driven Frankie to the *'Dirección General de la Guardia Civil'* in Marbella. He urgently needed to speak to the *'Comandante'* about some drugs he'd been offered … a large quantity of drugs! After half an hour of trying to explain at the front desk, he finally got to speak with an anti-narcotic

Teniente', who upon hearing the story, immediately summoned his superior. They ushered the Englishman into a secure office, at the rear of the building and closed the door. From just the little they'd heard already; this had all the hallmarks of being a large operation.

Three hours later, Frankie was back at the villa. Other than go over the plans, he could do no more until he made the 'phone calls' the next day.

It was going to be a long night!

***

In his room, Lamb read the latest e-mail, from 'mossad@mail.gov.il'

'(36.7 - 3.8) HRH Alfonso X1V-X1'

It wasn't too difficult to decipher;
   a. They'd confirmed the co-ordinates for Nerja
   b. A bronze statue of King Alfonzo stood on the 'Balcon de Europe' which was the suggested meeting point
   c. The X1V were the roman numerals for 14, the date for the meeting
   d. The X1 would be the time, 11 o'clock

He hoped!

It needed no reply, so he made his way out to the terrace for a late lunch and drinks. 'Afternoon Frankie, how did everything go today?'

'Ok it's all set for tomorrow'

'Have you spoken to Billy? do you reckon they fell for it and saw the map?'

Frankie nodded 'Yes, I had a word with him not long back, he's pretty sure they did. He was watching from inside; the older guy definitely used his phone's camera'

'Where's Billy now?'

'He's gone to brief the two Scottish lads and show them where their tools are stashed, as well as the routes they'll be taking in and out' he slapped Lamb on the back 'You're a right Julius Caesar Lamby'

Lamb smiled at the cockney rhyme for geezer', Frankie was obviously feeling better about life.

'Either that or I'm radio rental mate'

They both laughed breaking the tension as Frankie poured generous measures of Hendricks over ice and cucumber 'Oh sorry Lamby you don't like cucumber, do you?'

***

It was almost 10pm when Billy re-appeared, red faced and sweating 'Get me a drink Lamby mate and I'll brief you both on tomorrows arrangements. He walked towards the swimming pool, leaned down and scooped up handfuls of water to splash onto his face and into his hair 'Like a bloody furnace out there today'

Lamb returned with a tray holding a freshly made jug of sangria and three glasses, Betty had as usual, anticipated their needs. He walked over and placed it on the marble table 'This'll do for starters eh lads'

They waited for Billy to gulp down the first glass and pour himself another 'Sorry gents but it really was hot in those hills but I'm feeling better now'

Lamb was the first to speak 'Well, it's definitely happening tomorrow, so go-ahead Billy ... first off, tell us where we are with the goatherd's place ... the finca'

Billy took out a map, unfolded it and pointed to a red circle 'This is the same as I gave Jocie. As you know, this is the building, here' he looked at Lamb 'All the Modifications have been completed, as per your request ... Bert did a cracking job, you wouldn't think anyone had been near it for years' he paused for approval.

'Cheers Billy, thanks for that, now tell us how the Jocks are doing'

'Ok, here's what I've been sorting. Laird and Ghille the two Scottish' lads, have been shown their positions and after a couple of minor adjustments are happy with them, … they've also checked and cleaned their tools and are satisfied with them too' he looked at the others. 'So … I've informed them, that tomorrow evening, you and Frankie will pick them up in plenty of time to get sorted … me Johnny and Jocie, will then arrive up there a short while later'

Lamb looked up at his companions 'Ok, sounds good to me Billy, what do you reckon so far Frankie?

Frankie was just taking a sip of his Sangria, so just gave the thumbs up,

Lamb queried 'What happens to them afterwards Billy?'

Billy was in his stride now. 'Once they've completed their job, they'll bury their stuff and walk down to Johnny. He'll already have their travel kit in the motor and will take them to Marbella bus station. From there they can commence their journey north towards France, like any other tartan travellers' he laughed 'Although knowing them they'll probably have a few adventures on the way'

'Good so far Billy, now go through the timings'

Billy pulled out a notebook 'Ok … the timings have all been checked, that's why I was back late'. He

222

took a deep breath and continued 'The sun will begin to set where we want it, at 20.50hrs and will be to our maximum advantage at 20.58, that gives us an eight-minute window' he looked at Frankie 'I've driven the route twice. ... Frankie, you'll need to call your new mates at 20.35' he looked up to be certain Frankie had heard him 'You'll then need to make your second call by 20.45 latest'

Lamb smiled 'Good work Billy, we'll synchronise watches in the morning'

Frankie interjected 'That just leaves the shirts, how can we be absolutely sure they'll play ball'

It was Lamb that answered 'As you were aware, this plan could always go in one of two directions'

'First case scenario; the shirts could use what they've seen on the map to set up an ambush at the finca. ...We are aware of that possibility and if that is what they do, our Scottish friends will be on hand to alert us to it! ... ... In that case, Jocie won't need to have any further involvement'

Frankie poured the last of the Sangria 'Go on'

'Second case scenario; and the one I favour. ... They could wait until tomorrow evening, then follow Jocie from the hotel, out to the finca and attack us there! ... After all, they think it's only going to be Frankie and her, or, Frankie, me and her, at the meeting'. He paused 'I'm pretty certain, this will be their chosen option'

Frankie looked at Lamb 'What makes you so certain it's the second option, the night's not over yet?'

'Good question … tell me Billy, do you know if they've been out of the hotel and driven anywhere this afternoon or evening?'

Billy shook his head 'No, we've had eyes on them since they followed Johnny back from the airport and then watched me and Jocie at the Belvedere. All they've done, is have a meal and knock a few drinks back, especially the younger one. The lads would have phoned me if they'd moved'

Lamb glanced at both the others in turn, to get his point across. 'Being pro's, we'd have expected them to have already gone out and done a recce of the area. It would need to be in daylight, just to get the lay of the land and it would only need to be a quick drive-by. … They haven't … so … that suggests to me, either the photos they took of the map didn't work out, … or … they're worried they might give the game away, if we saw them nosing around out there!' He hesitated 'I'm convinced they already believe Jocie will be picked up and taken to the meeting place tomorrow evening … and I'm also certain they'll follow her' his companions nodded. 'So, Billy, both you and Johnny will pick her up for safety reasons' he looked at his friend 'Billy, you can see why it has to be you who fetches her. If Frankie or I, or worse still, both, went to get her, they might just decide to take us all out on the road, … before we even got to the finca'

Billy smiled understandingly 'Ok I can see what you're getting at, they're not going to do anything to me Johnny and Jocie, until they're sure. at least one of you two is out at the finca'

Frankie put his hand up 'It sounds logical to me'

Billy nodded 'Carry on Lamb I'm listening'

Lamb then went over the rest of the plan in fine detail 'Okay any questions?

Frankie took the opportunity to express his concerns 'Just one, for Billy, these phone calls I'm to make, are we sure there's a signal'

Lamb patted him on the back 'Damn good question mate … Billy?'

'Yes, we checked when we first went looking for the location and I've been checking ever since.

Lamb smiled 'Good, those phone calls are the most important part of the plan, if that goes wrong, nothing else will work and everyone will be in danger'

Billy jumped in again 'I forgot to mention, any equipment the Scots lads stash will be retrieved eight to ten days later. Once things have cooled down'

Lamb glanced towards the villa 'Now all we need is a volunteer for the next part …'

225

Frankie and Billy looked at him enquiringly.

He pointed at the jug 'We need a refill and I got the last one!'

Frankie laughed 'Bugger the fruit juice its Brandy time'

***

Day 17 … Friday 13th May 2016

Unlucky for some!

The immigration officer at Malaga airport barely glanced at Elise and Lucas Maes's Belgian passports, before sourly nodding at them to proceed. He was just beginning a double shift, thanks to a colleague calling in sick, so was in a foul mood. It didn't matter; he could never have known the full details of their earlier travel arrangements. He couldn't have known for instance; that they'd initially flown to Athens from Tel-Aviv's Ben Gurion airport with Aegean Airlines. That they'd briefly left the airport during the short two-hour stopover. And that they'd returned to board a Vueling flight for their onward journey to Malaga. That break certainly couldn't have been for sightseeing, there was barely enough time to exit the terminal and check in again! Stepped out for a desperately needed cigarette? Maybe, but doubtful, there was a total absence of tobacco odour on them. He could though, have been curious about the very small suitcases they pulled and why they only had one-way tickets. However, he wasn't curious about anything, he was just pissed off! He was miffed that he wouldn't now be going to the atmospheric 'Antigua Casa de Guardia' where he would sip small glasses of strong Malaga wines or the 'Fabrica' a Cruzcampo bar with onstage entertainment. It was where he and his *amigos* went every Friday!

There was nothing to distinguish the Israeli pair, whose real names were Romi Kadosh and Shimon Stern, from any other young married couple on holiday. Both could be described as career professionals, both in their early thirties and both wearing smart but non-designer casual wear. They'd be un-noticeable in any crowd.

When they'd stepped outside the terminal in Athens, they'd used a slick and well-practised manoeuvre, to exchange their Israeli passports for forged Belgian ones. They'd also swapped their original suitcases for identical ones containing French and Belgian labelled items,

Intriguingly both were also members of an Israeli Mossad 'Kidon' team, honouring their motto;

'By way of deception thou shalt do war'

Two other Israeli team members arrived in Spain that day. Shizaf Levi and Alon Dayon had both disembarked from the El-Al direct flight from Tel-Aviv to Madrid, supposedly to look at Spanish furniture export opportunities. On arrival, they'd made their way to Calle Velázquez to pick up false Dutch passports, driving licences and various credit cards in the names of Sem Van Dijk and Luuk Bakker. Also supplied to them, was a large Weinsberg Carasuite motor home registered in their names, and a few pieces of specialist equipment. These were four 9mm Glock 19 semi-automatic hand guns with suppressors, the favoured weapon of this particular group. Now their cover story was exploring holiday destinations on Spain's Costa del Sol

Having completed that part of their mission, both men then wasted no time in making their way towards an overnight stay in the beautiful Spa town of 'Alhama de Granada' midway between Granada and Malaga. Soon they would make their way to Nerja, where they hoped to solve a mystery involving someone code named 'Matador' an 'Iranian hitman' and some 'obsolete Nuclear Missiles!'

Retribution opened its gates; the gladiators were entering the arena!

***

Following the success of the previous day, Edward Warling and Filip Wojtek rewarded themselves with a late breakfast at their luxury hotel. After examining the images taken on Edward's mobile phone, they now had a definite plan for the day ahead.

The previous night, Filip had driven over to the nearby Park Plaza Suites Hotel to check up on the reporter woman. At the same time, he'd parked and left their 4 x 4 there, in readiness for this evenings' business. Now, examining the section of map they could see on the mobile, they'd have plenty of time to clean and prepare their weapons, before relaxing at a nearby bar.

Strictly teetotal of course, they were after all professionals!

Whilst Filip was on his mission, Edward Warling contacted Pontin and gave him an update on recent events and the change of plan from the 14th to the 13th.

'The arrival of the reporter couldn't have worked better for myself and Filip. By arranging to meet with her; Lamb and his gangster friend have built their own trap' he let it sink in, revelling in his own smugness. 'It merely needs to be sprung, after that they will no longer be a threat' He continued, eager to impress his boss. 'You can be assured; the targets will soon be eliminated!' His confidence rose '*After* their bodies have been discovered … but not before, we will deliberately leak rumours. These will imply that she had threatened to expose the gangster's past sexual indiscretions'

Pontin liked a good fairy-tale

Warling continued to expand his plot. 'Evidence will indicate that it had all gone tragically wrong, when in a rage, Lane had fatally shot her!' he paused for effect 'Finally, the prospect of being jailed for murder, combined with the emotional stress to his terminally ill wife, will have proven too much for him … so he committed suicide'.

Pontin voiced his approval 'Not a perfect story, but almost impossible to challenge, carry on Edward'

Encouraged Warling replied 'There were certain facts in our favour' he listed them;
'A witness friend of ours, will have seen a man resembling Lane, in a red baseball cap. He'd been at the hotel in deep conversation with the woman and was also seen to hand her a map'
'The same witness, will have seen her getting picked up by the same man quite late into the evening and being driven away from her hotel'
'Both a map and a red baseball cap, would be found in his vehicle at the crime scene'
'His devotion to his wife is legendary, so any personal scandal would obviously be unbearable for him'

'What about the Spanish? Pontin asked

Warling answered 'Few enquiries would be made by the Spanish authorities. After all, Lane is known in England as a former criminal and who the press once called a 'hard man and a drug dealer'

'And Lamb?'

'If Lamb is there, he will first be taken elsewhere, for 'intimate debriefing'. If not, then we can assume he's heading for his own fateful demise in Nerja. Harkant or the Iranian will deal with him and Filip and I will track him from this end, just to make sure. Either way it will be over very soon'.

He smiled at his own cunning and ended the phone call.

Some ten minutes later, Warling walked to the balcony of his apartment and looked out towards the sea. His eyes were drawn to the ghost like appearance of a huge white cruise liner, near to the horizon. It was a vast floating edifice carrying some 3,000 souls. In his mind, most of those on board were retirees, dragging out the last of life's memories whilst dribbling gin and tonic and other foodstuffs into their laps. That he'd never been on a cruise ship and couldn't have been more mistaken didn't bother him. He'd always been an opinionated snob, and saw himself in his mind's eye, sitting at the captain's table. He'd be wearing a black bowtie and white tuxedo jacket whilst sneering at those below his station. He also imagined that with a mere click of his fingers he could manipulate anyone on board, including the crew. In a moment of uncharacteristic melancholy, he smiled inwardly,

Maybe when this mission was over, he might just go to sea!

Wojtek returned to the hotel after a short stroll to check up on the X5. He wasn't going to return to his room just yet, they had plenty of time to kill. He smiled at those words; 'time to kill' it was one of his favourite English sayings. Today was to be a good day, it would culminate in the use of his specialist skills, practised over and over again in the Branch's exclusive training range.

No one could put bullets into a person with the precision he possessed. It wasn't easy to make both a murder and a suicide believable to modern forensic investigations. There were all manner of things to take into account; powder residue, blood spatter, point of entry, angle of discharge, range, even the placement of the spent cartridges. Both murder and suicide each had their own separate considerations. A special courier had already delivered the weapon to be used. It was a pretty standard and very common Army Issue Browning 9mm semi-automatic pistol. Having been in production since before world war two, they were the model of gun aging gangsters would have lying around, … from the 'good old times'

It would be messy but effective, and today was to be a good day!

***

Mr Churchill groaned; he'd not been enjoying his boring breakfast of half a Cantaloupe with Cottage cheese and a garnish of parsley. It was prescribed on the advice of his dietician, who was puzzled by the steady rise of his cholesterol levels. The phone call wasn't softening his mood either 'So your telling me that this is it, the end, no more, it's over eh Pontin?'

He laughed sarcastically 'Of course, those braindead dimwits of yours would say that wouldn't they' his anger spilled out 'No! I do not want to hear any more details!' His voice rose a few more octaves 'This has been going on for over two weeks now … and in that time you've managed to get an American killed … and … God knows how you achieved it so quickly … make us the laughing stock in front of them' he cut short the protests on the other end of the call 'For God's sake can you honestly guarantee me that we can put this whole miserable episode behind us after today?' He slammed his fist on the desk top 'Pontin, ninety percent is not a guarantee! It's not even bloody close!' He spoke resignedly 'Just get it right this time ok! For both our sakes, our futures depend on it' He slammed the phone down on the desk then picked up his meal and threw it in the bin 'Jesus Christ, the crap I have to swallow for my country'

The red phone burst into life 'Hello Mr Lincoln I was just thinking of you'

***

      Lamb rose early, he hadn't slept particularly well, there were too many details swirling around in his head. After a shower, he dressed in sand coloured Chinos and beige polo shirt, not exactly camouflage, but more than adequate for the day's events. He walked out to the patio where Betty was laying out breakfast 'Morning Betty how are you?' he put his arm around her shoulders 'Is Frankie up?'

235

She stepped away and turned to look at him 'Yes he is' she hesitated 'Martin I don't know the details of what's happening today and I don't want to … I certainly know better than to ask Francis … but I'm not blind, I do know something serious is going on … and I want you to swear to me that you'll look after him … I mean it Martin … I want you to swear that you'll do that!'

He could see in her eyes a complex mixture of devotion and pride. There was also anger at the man she'd been with for most of her life who was now putting her through this. He also sensed in her a fear that Frankie might die before her and leave her behind. It was that thought that terrified her the most. He held her close in reassurance 'Betty I swear I'll look after him … at no time will he be in a position of danger, Billy and I will make sure of that'

'And you Martin will you be in a position of danger?'

'Possibly, but it isn't the same with me, today is something that I have to see through'

'But why danger? that's not the same as taking a risk and you know it, is there no other way for you?'

He still had his hands on her shoulders 'Betty, you and Frankie have something very special, it's what Mary and I had. After I lost her, I came here to Spain to find her again through memories' he looked away before she could see the rage in his eyes. 'Those bastards even took that away from me' he took a deep breath 'Others call it danger Betty, but to me it's an unbreakable cord that ties me to them. … It stops them escaping from the justice they deserve!' He looked for understanding 'The corrupt people in power send their killers to crush the decent people of this world and that will never change!' He tried to control his anger 'But this time we'll send them a message … not here and not us!'

She reached out to place her hand on his arm 'You scare me with your anger Martin and although I think I understand, you have to consider your children'. She watched him, as his mind fought against the unlocking of a deep personal vault 'You don't have the right to just cut them out of your life, it's their decision as well'. She gripped his arm tighter 'Martin you gave them that decision the second they were born!'

He knew she was right, but until this was sorted, his only ambition was the total destruction of those who murder innocents, in the name of governance! He sighed with relief as the vault slammed shut again 'One-day Betty, … maybe one day'

'Morning Lamby you trying to chat up my Betty out here?' Frankie laughed 'Only joking mate, how you feeling?' he leaned over and kissed his wife. 'You didn't need to lay out the breakfast this morning, I know how busy you are today. Us lads have got some serious talking to do but we'd have coped'

She laughed 'You need more than coffee and Brandy to start the day … and I mean all of you!'

She looked at Lamb. 'Now I do have to get ready for my trip to England and Tommy's funeral, the taxi will be here soon. She smiled 'So remember what I said' she put her finger to her lips and looked across at her husband 'And if he asks you what I mean, tell him to mind his own business'

Frankie laughed 'Don't worry I know better than to ask' he walked towards the balustrade overlooking the town below 'Billy's up and on his way, he decided to WhatsApp Jocie to confirm the arrangements last night' he winked, 'I reckon they've got a soft spot for each other'. Anyway, when he gets here, I'd like to run through everything just one more time'.

Lamb smiled 'Good on them, I hope they do get it together after this is over' he moved his tongue over the loose tooth, 'Might calm Billy down a bit'

One hour later, with breakfast over and the plans confirmed with Billy and Frankie, Lamb stood on the front terrace looking over the roof tops towards the sea. On the horizon he could just see a large white cruise liner and it released a deluge of emotions in him. His knuckles turned white as he gripped the balustrade, anger and sadness fought each other to conquer his mind.

Frankie gripped his arm 'You ok Lamby? you've gone a bit pale'

238

Lamb turned away embarrassed by his watery eyes. The tension of the previous two weeks was being replaced by the pain of deep sorrow. 'I'm okay mate, only Mary always fancied a cruise and seeing that ship kinda brought it back'. He turned and faced his friend 'I'm sorry Frankie you've got your own troubles I didn't mean to… '

Frankie raised his hand 'Forget it mate I'm ok'

Billy walked over to them and all three looked to the horizon deep in their own thoughts. They knew that by the end of the day their lives will have changed irreversibly!

They would lock arms with Fate and face the Devil!

***

In Nerja, a young Belgian' couple, checked into the welcoming Hostal Alegre on avenue de Pescia, dumped their cases and went for a walk. They held hands as any devoted pair might do but this wasn't an act of passion, this was business! They were highly trained scouts and they were looking for two things; potential threats and an Iranian called Albazi Hashimi. If either of them spotted anything of interest, they would use a squeeze code to alert and direct the others' attention, without anyone near them noticing. It was also quicker for one partner to pull the other out of harm's way, if they encountered immediate danger.

The milliseconds saved by not having to explain could be the difference between life and death.

Tomorrow two colleagues would join them, at what level of alertness would depend on the message they sent today.

The two Dutch' men, parked the camper van on the outskirts of Alhama de Granada, locked the doors and unpacked the four 9mm semi-automatics. They then stripped them down and wiped off the protective coating of light oil. After re-assembling them and checking the action of each gun, they similarly cleaned and loaded the 8 magazines with the ammunition supplied. Being professionals, they didn't fill the magazines to full capacity, it was better to under fill them by one round as it reduced the chances of the gun jamming. One man then went down the main street and walked around the block to dump the cleaning cloths and various wrappers. Whilst away his companion brewed two cups of strong expresso coffee, to disguise the distinctive sweet smell of gun oil, nothing was left to chance!

They were currently ignorant of the looming apocalypse in the hills above Puerto Banus and the impact it would ultimately have on their own lives'

***

Day 17 … Friday 13th May 2016 … (pm)

'War is mainly a catalogue of blunders' …
Winston Churchill

Martin Lamb, Frankie Lane and the two Scotsmen, Laird Caithstead and Ghille Jock climbed into the white Range Rover. They then made their way out to the valley, behind the goatherd's finca. Once past it, but still in the vicinity, both Scots were dropped off, to climb up to their respective vantage points, on opposing sides of the valley. Each had a clear view of the rear of the finca and more importantly, they could also see the track leading to the front of it. Both Caithstead and Jock, then removed some small boulders and scraped away the soil to reveal long canvas bags. Opening their bag, they each extracted a second-hand Spanish Bergara B14 Woodsman rifle, preloaded with a magazine of three rounds and telescopic sight. Also, in each bag were four additional magazines, all holding three bullets, a small facecloth, four bottles of water, a pair of black leather gloves and a small two-way radio. After putting on the gloves, they checked their gun's working parts for smoothness of operation, then sprinkled dust over the front lens of the telescopic sight. This latter action was to minimise any reflection from the lens, whilst still leaving it clear enough to see through. They then made themselves comfortable by lying on the canvas bags and settled down to await the arrival of their targets and the commencement of the mission.

Meanwhile, Frankie and Lamb parked the 4 x 4 out of sight further down the valley, before making their way back up the hill, to the rear of the finca. They were each carrying a small two-way radio and were listening for any alerts from the Scots. Once at the finca, Lamb pulled on a particularly rough piece of plaster low down on the back wall. This allowed a section of the wall to come away revealing a hole, large enough for a person to enter the building on all fours, unseen by anyone at the front.

Bert 'The Chippy' had done this part of his job extremely well!

Inside the finca, they could see on the old chest of drawers a square parcel wrapped in black Guerrilla tape. On top of that, was a small Uzi machine pistol that had been recently fired, its magazine was only half full, which was reflected by the empty shell casings lying on the dusty floor,

Billy had indeed been busy the previous evening!

Beneath the small window, was a rusty bedframe, on which Lamb stood to watch the track out front, as they waited for Johnny to drop off Billy and Jocie.

Frankie made his first phone call.

It was to the Guardia Civil *Teniente* and he informed him that the Drug Dealers had given him an approximate area to go to. He suggested that he might wish to deploy his men nearer to this area whilst they awaited final instructions.

The battle lines were drawn!

Billy, wearing his red baseball cap and Johnny, drove down to the Park Plaza hotel to pick up Jocie, then continued up towards the hills and the goatherd's finca. They already knew that the Shirts' black X5 was in the carpark because Johnny had visited it during the early hours of that morning.

He'd been applying his specialist skills during a nocturnal mission for Lamb.

When they reached the track that led to the finca, Johnny halted the vehicle to let Billy escort Jocie down to it. Both walked slowly and were met at the door by Frankie and Lamb. Billy then returned to Johnny and both drove off in the direction they'd already been travelling.

Wojtek was finding Edward Warling really annoying. Firstly, because he Filip' had not had a drink all day and secondly because Warling was wearing a particularly smug expression.

'Didn't I tell you all along Filip that the reporter woman would lead us to our gangster?' he looked across at his travelling companion. 'Who knows, you might even get to amuse yourself with her before we are finished, would that make you happier my boy?'

Wojtek shrugged, he hated the condescending way Warling dished out favours, as though they were his alone to give. If he wanted to amuse himself, he would, he didn't need Warling's permission. He thought about it and decided he quite liked the idea; they'd blame it on the gangster anyway.

They'd followed the white Mercedes saloon ever since it had left the hotel with the reporter. Now they were keeping sufficient distance from it, so as not to be seen by the three occupants. When it stopped at the entrance of a track, Warling grabbed his small self-focusing binoculars, stepped out of the X5 and climbed up to the top of a small mound. From there he could see the man in the red baseball cap and the woman walking down the track, towards a small finca, and his breath caught in his throat!

He could see the heads of two more men, he checked again then suppressed a laugh, it was both Lamb and Lane!

As Lamb, Lane and the reporter entered the finca, the man in the red baseball cap returned to the vehicle which then drove off. Warling was un-characteristically trembling with excitement, as he returned to tell his friend Filip.

The enemy were at the gates!

The fourteen Guardia Civil and Police anti-narcotics officers, along with a paramedic, climbed into their vehicles and drove closer to the area indicated by Frankie Lane. They hadn't launched the force helicopter at this stage, as not knowing exactly where the dealers were, there was a good chance it might alert them. Apart from the paramedic, each officer was armed with a Heckler & Koch USP 9mm pistol and a H&K MP5 9mm automatic rifle.

Firepower wasn't in short supply!

From now on they would stay seated in their vehicles, on standby, ready to move at a moment's notice.

Up on the high ridges, the two Scotsmen, radioed in a sitrep'. They'd just observed the black BMW X5 advance slowly along the track before parking up behind a tree lined hillock. They then watched as the two occupants disembarked and cautiously made their way towards the finca. Each had a small black pistol in his hand. Caithstead extracted a round from the magazine, as he drew back the bolt of his rifle. He then chambered it by sliding the bolt forward and clicking it down firmly. Ghille Jock carried out the same procedure. Next, both men placed a facecloth over the end of their rifle barrel, this would hide the tell-tale muzzle flash and suppress some of the sound. Using the water from the bottles they soaked the cloths; the wetness would both stop the cloth from flying off and also prevent it from catching alight. It was a simple procedure but effective. Their first shot would be into the ground to the side of the target, the resultant dust flume would show them how accurate the sights were and allow them to compensate.

After all they didn't want to hurt anyone!

Lamb, Lane and Jocie Bell had been tipped off by the Scots as soon as the shirts parked up. Frankie made his second phone call, before all three crawled out of the finca through the hole in the back wall. Lamb then carefully replaced the false panel and jammed it shut using a deliberately placed old rusty iron bar and some strategically positioned rocks. Anyone examining the finca either externally or internally wouldn't spot Bert's masterpiece of deception. They then made their way down the valley covered by the two sharpshooters in the hills either side.

Both shirts shaded their eyes against the sun's glare and cautiously advanced towards the finca. Each had a round chambered in their semi-automatic and the safety catch off. One covered the window whilst the other watched the door, ready to react instantly to any threat that might suddenly present itself. Neither spoke as Warling signalled to Wojtek to cover him. He then leaned with his back against the wall and gently placed his left hand on the door handle in readiness. After a confirmation nod from his companion and in a single smooth action born of much training, Warling shoved down on the latch and burst into the room. Whilst he crouched low to cover the right-hand space behind the door Wojtek followed immediately, staying tall to cover the area to the left. Both men looked at each other in puzzlement at the absence of targets, before Warling crossed to the rickety chest of drawers and examined the items on top. At the same time, the spring-loaded door gently clicked shut behind them … *Bert's handiwork continued to impress!*

Wojtek turned to open the door and guard against attack but was surprised to find there was no interior handle, nor could he see it anywhere in the immediate vicinity.

Come into my parlour said the spider to the fly!

Warling meanwhile, had moved the Uzi machine pistol off on top of the parcel and was tearing at the tape to examine the contents. At the back of his mind alarm bells were ringing. They turned to church bells as the crack of bullets sounded close-by and several thudded into the outside walls!

Frankie's second call had given the Guardia Civil *Teniente* the precise location of the proposed drug deal. This was supposedly provided to him by the drug dealers.

Within minutes the squad reached the track leading down to the finca. They climbed out of their vehicles and advanced on foot. They'd walked just a few metres when bullets suddenly cracked overhead, others kicked up dust and stones around them. They appeared to be coming from the small white building to their front. Precise target recognition was impossible as the powerful glare from the sunset behind the finca was blinding. However, they had no reason to think they were coming from anywhere else!

As the officers dived for cover, the order was given to return fire!

Twenty-two 9mm Parabellum rounds splintered through the door of the finca in the first seven seconds, whilst another forty pounded into the walls and through the window.

Fate was copper clad ... and it didn't knock!

Caithstead and Jock stuck to their mission and fired their first rounds, close to and then into, the walls of the building. This achieved their intended aim and startled the shirts into believing they were being ambushed by Lamb and his crew. Then, with the sun continuing to set behind them, the two marksmen concentrated their shots, over the roof towards, but not directly at, the law enforcement squad. This convinced the officers that the occupants inside were responsible and induced them to return fire.

Events were now escalating rapidly, and within two minutes the advantage of the sun's glare would be gone. Aware of this, the Scots calmly used what remaining ammunition they had, then rolled over out of sight, to pick up their expended cartridge cases. It was a job well done! After wiping clean their weapons, they pocketed the face cloth, then put everything except the water bottles they'd drank from, into the canvas bags. These they re-buried for collection at a later date. Keeping low, they then made their way back down to Johnny and the waiting car. Their part of the operation was now over and it had been completed with no further questions asked. It was no less than what Frankie or any of the others would have done for them.

No payment was offered nor asked for, there was indeed still honour among thieves!

Whilst Johnny drove the two Scotsmen to Marbella bus station, Billy drove Lamb, Frankie and Jocie back to the villa. The sound of automatic gunfire, followed by an explosion told them all they needed to know. There was no point in hanging around. No-one spoke, they were neither happy nor sad, merely satisfied. The shirts had brought this upon themselves, they had killed their friends, so be it, now they were paying the piper.

Nor was it over yet, as part of the same plan, Jocie would begin to write a news story.

Lamb though, still had unfinished business in Nerja!

***

Back at the finca events had come to a bloody conclusion:

In response to the initial shots being fired by the Scots, a desperate Warling climbed onto the bedframe and fired blindly through the window, trying to buy time. Furiously, Wojtek continued to barge the door, in an attempt to escape the trap:

20.56pm ... Filip Wojtek would never amuse himself with anyone again, his wasn't a good day after all ...!

In frustration, at the door not opening, he fired 5 shots at the lock in a futile attempt to break it. Within seconds, he himself was hit six times as police bullets punched through the woodwork.

It was the fifth slug that killed him, shattering a rib before ricocheting through his heart and severing two vertebrae. He died in a sitting position on the dirt floor with his eyes wide open, in an expression of incomprehension and rage.

20.57pm ... Edward Warling would never go to sea, he didn't die, but would later wish he had!

Three bullets came through the window and slammed into him. The first hit his gun before taking away the thumb from his right hand. The second destroyed his left shoulder blade before exiting through his upper arm and the final one, took away a large part of his lower jaw. Unbalanced from his perch on the bedstead, his right leg plunged down through the rusty bed-springs which held it tight. His Tibia and Fibula both then snapped as he crashed sideways into the chest of drawers, dislodging the drugs package on his way down to the floor. Seconds later, his eardrums burst and he was temporarily blinded as a stun grenade came through the window. A huge cloud of dust and cocaine swirled around him as he passed out and he never heard nor saw the black clad figures bursting through the door. Their fingers were on the triggers, ready to fire if either suspect should do so much as blink!

Ironically, the third bullet that rendered him unconscious, probably also saved his life!

***

Day 18 … Saturday 14th May 2016

In memoriam …

Lamb was the first to rise followed by Billy, who joined him at the balustrade overlooking the town.

'Morning Billy, how are you feeling this morning mate?'

Billy ran his fingers through his unkempt hair 'Morning Lamb, ok thanks, anyway as you're off to Nerja today Frankie and me reckon I should be going with you. We still don't know where the American is and you've also got the Iraqi to contend with, things could get tasty!'

Lamb nodded 'Thanks buddy, I will need you to drive me out to Nerja, but after that, I'm going to need professional help and that's not an insult to you and Frankie by the way. I'll explain what I mean when he's here.

Ten minutes later, Frankie joined them and Lamb explained his plan to both men over breakfast. Billy and Lamb then climbed into the Range Rover and journeyed towards Nerja.

Neither carried weapons of any sort, that would be the responsibility of others!

Back at the villa, *Capitan* Luis Munoz of the Spanish police, arrived to brief Frankie on the preceding day's events;

'Our officers found the handle for the inside of the door lock under dirt in the far corner of the room. We don't know why this should be so! Also, an initial search of the finca and both suspects, has revealed the following' he read from a list;

'2 Taurus Curve pistols which had both been fired before one had sustained damage'

'3 empty magazines and 3 full ones, each containing 6 rounds'

'An old 9mm Browning pistol with a magazine of 12 bullets, this had Wojtek's fingerprints on it'

'An Uzi machine pistol that also had Warling's fingerprints on it. This had recently been used and was partially jammed so it could only fire single shots. This explained the initial low rate of inaccurate fire aimed at the officers'

'A ripped package that had Warling's fingerprints on it containing Cocaine, with an estimated street value of around €60,000'

He paused as Frankie absorbed the details

'In the BMW X5 they also found'
'An envelope containing €38,000 in cash under the driver's seat, the notes also had traces of cocaine on them that matched the narcotics haul'
'On the floor, behind the front passenger seat, along with a new red baseball cap, was a map with a red circle drawn on it. The circle coincided with the location of the finca' the red crayon that drew it, was in the glovebox'

Legend had it, that there wasn't a vehicle that Johnny 'The chauffeur' Kinsel couldn't break into, and he'd applied those skills to great effect during his recent nocturnal activity.

The *Capitan* continued 'Subsequent checks on the suspects passports have revealed them to be fake. A request by the Spanish Police, to the United Kingdom's Border Force, revealed there was no record of them having ever been issued. That knowledge and the suspicious way they frequently changed hotels, points to them being drug dealers trying to enter the Spanish narcotics market!' He paused 'One other thing that concerned us, was the specialist nature of the two Taurus pistols. They are an unusual choice of weapon and suggest the owners held a high rank in whichever cartel they represented'.

'Another small concern of ours, Mr Lane, is that the suspect's mobile phones show no trace of the calls made to you, regarding the locations for the meeting. We have therefore concluded, that there must have been a third suspect. Probably someone junior in the organisation, who was just paid to make the calls. An examination of your mobile virtually confirms this, as there are indeed two calls from an unknown source'

The officer concluded his briefing with the following comment.

Thanks to the bravery of you, Mr Lane, a gang, that could potentially have imported millions of euros' worth of drugs into Spain, has been prevented from doing so!' He paused 'Normally such an action would have warranted an award, in recognition of our country's gratitude. However, the high risk of retribution if you were to be identified, make this not possible. Maybe there was another way we could reward you'

***

In Nerja, Lyndon Harkant was both mourning and smarting. The former, at the loss of his partner eight days previously. The latter, at the instructions he'd received from 'Cassidy' his boss, back at Scope's head office in Langley Virginia, He'd just finished his breakfast in the Trebol restaurant and was now staring at the fountain in the centre of the road, contemplating his next move. He'd heard nothing from the Brits so figured they'd be chasing their own butts in one way or another. Anyway, he was pretty sure they'd contact him if anything important developed. Sergio's funeral service was due to start at 7pm that evening, that's when he hoped to have his first contact with Lamb. Cassidy though, had told him to 'back off' from the Brit! He was to leave it to the Iranian, who still wasn't aware of the American's involvement, never mind his presence in Nerja. Predictably, Hashimi would now be knocking back Brandys, whilst watching the Quixote bar, along with any young women that strayed into his radar. Cassidy had said things were getting out of hand and it was only a matter of time, before the whole thing exploded in a mess of publicity. He knew the head shed was basically telling him that he'd failed, but he wasn't done yet! The feel of the Sig Sauer in his specially reinforced pocket, gave him some comfort. He forced a grim smile at the thought of showing Lamb how it worked. The limey had killed Jaycee and orders or not, he wasn't going to let that go unpunished; they could go to hell.

Retribution knocked on Satan's gate … he should prepare for a visitor!

* * *

Lamb asked to be dropped off at Plaza de Cavana, after reassuring Billy of his safety or the tenth time. He then walked past the seventeenth century

258

Church of El Salvador, to secure himself a table at the Kronox restaurant. Satisfied with his view over the Balcon and comfortable in the knowledge that he blended in with the many customers, he ordered a small beer and settled back to watch for his soon to be allies. He was also confident that his enemies wouldn't dare try anything in this location. The time was approaching midday as he ordered another beer and a toastie for lunch. He paid when they arrived, in case he should need to move suddenly.

Although he couldn't actually see the bronze statue of King Alfonso, he didn't mind as the people he was due to contact wouldn't be standing next to it. He was certain, that like him, they'd also be on the periphery observing everyone.

Just before half past one he noticed the two men: They'd been together as they walked past the church, but once on the square they'd separated and were now making their way along the Balcon on opposite sides. They were both taking photographs, of everything unimportant.

He'd decided not to make his move until the meeting time of two o'clock had passed. This was to gauge not only the two men's reactions, but those of someone else. Standing beneath the arches were a youngish couple, they were holding hands and looking in the direction of the square and the church, that in itself wasn't cause for caution.

What was suspicious however; is that they'd been doing so for twenty-five minutes and had never once turned around to look at the stunning sea and mountain views, unlike all the other tourists!

His phone pinged to notify him that he'd received an e-mail, but he ignored it. He saw all four of those he was watching, scan their allocated areas for anyone suddenly checking their phone. It wasn't exactly a sophisticated ploy, but in certain situations it could be effective. However, this time it had worked against them. He'd noticed the male with the woman tapping into his mobile just prior to the message being received. At ten minutes past two he made his move, not towards the Bronze statue but towards the young couple under the arches.

He walked past them and leaned over the railings to look down at the sunbathers enjoying Calahonda beach below. After a few minutes he approached them from behind and spoke quietly 'Excuse me but do you speak English?'

The woman turned, eying him suspiciously 'Yes, a little, but why do you ask?'

He smiled and showed them a map of Nerja, torn from the latest copy of SolTal; across the top in small handwriting was;

'M1003 (MGM-31C) - (SS-1d) Modification Requirements'

'I'm looking for the statue of Alfonzo, do you know where it, I was told it was here somewhere?' he watched her read the message before nodding to her companion.

She spoke in perfect English but with a feint American accent, gained from her time studying 'Linguistics' at Cornell University 'We've been waiting Mr …?'

'Names later, first we need somewhere to talk' he looked over at the two males further up the Balcon, poised for action and waiting for a signal from the woman. 'Are you inviting your friends to the party?'

She raised her eyebrows then laughed 'No they'll follow and stay on high alert, we didn't know what to expect when we got your message … and you could still turn out to be a hoaxer … or a threat' it was a veiled warning, they were in control, she gestured with her arm 'Lead on mystery man'

He led them beneath the *Ayuntamiento*, past the tourism office, up towards Plaza de Espana and onto the terrace of the smart Hermes restaurant 'We'll be fine here for a couple of hours, there's a lot to talk about' he paused. 'But first I'll need you to give me your word, that you won't act upon the information, until I say so, … no matter how outrageous it might sound'

She started to protest but he cut her off 'Your word or we part company now … and don't make any threats, that would be a disaster for all of us!' He grinned 'This is a top-quality restaurant and it's my party you've come to, so you can bring the wine … let's have a bottle of Rioja Martelo 2012 … thanks'

261

Lamb told them in detail about 'Operation Bikini' and the deception planned by the UK, USA and Iraqi governments. He explained about his initial message and confirmed to them the link between the Pershing and Scud missiles and how he believed they were to be modified. He also explained how the countries involved, were now trying to kill him. The sd card and the 'Shirts' demise, were not mentioned, not yet anyway, that would come later.

The Israeli couple studied him intently, as though trying to decide if he was genuine, or just some nutter they were dealing with.

'If this is true show us some proof, I mean how do we know you've not made this whole thing up to cause trouble between us and our western allies. After all anyone can google most of what you just told us!'

He'd been expecting their response 'I can show you proof, and I will, but first I need an assurance that your country won't just go charging in. Not before I've explained, how best to make this work to all our advantages' there was only firmness in his voice now.

The woman eyed her companion then turned back to Lamb 'I'm sorry, but even with proof we can't give you the assurance you're asking for, that can only come from the Knesset'

He nodded, it was what he'd expected to hear, but he was merely showing them he had issues 'Ok I understand that but you see my point, I don't want you lot nuking someone before you've understood the potential benefits'

Both the Israelis laughed 'I can assure you Mr Lamb, our country would not just 'nuke' as you call it, anyone without very real justification, it would make us extremely unpopular'

'Ok but now you know how concerned I am' he looked around to check for eavesdroppers 'These are my requests, they are simple to implement, and of very little cost to yourselves'. The woman leaned forward in her seat as he continued, 'Firstly, I have a friend who needs a favour, he wants to return to England and it would be good if your country could help him achieve that' he paused, to gauge if they were taking him seriously. 'Once I reveal the full story to you, it's importance will become apparent'

'Go on Mr Lamb'

'Secondly, I wish to continue my life without having to look over my shoulder constantly. So, whilst I don't want protection, I would like certain assurances from the governments involved'

She nodded 'Rather like Israel itself, so we could hardly think that unreasonable'

'Finally, in order to hide their secret, they murdered two of my friends' he noted the immediate change in demeanour from the man and woman he was addressing 'I want justice for them' he again paused 'There are two people who I believe to be here in

Nerja right now, and both want to kill me' they were listening now, he could tell. 'An American agent called Lynden Harkant, who has killed before, and the Iraqi I sent you the picture of, though I know nothing else about him'

The woman spoke to her companion in Hebrew then turned to Lamb 'Our apologies for not speaking English, sometimes it is simpler for us to confer in Hebrew. Anyway, we have information on the Iraqi' you speak of, only he is not Iraqi, he is Iranian.' She let this sink in 'His name is Albazi Hashimi and he escaped to Turkey with his mother during the Iranian revolution in 1979. He then moved to Iraq when he was twenty' she noticed the sudden look of surprise on his face 'Why is that of significance Mr Lamb, what does it mean to you?'

'I lived in Iran for some years, working for the army as a technical adviser, just prior to the revolution, but why an Iranian and not an Iraqi, I'm confused'

'There are a few things we can tell you about him. For a start, he's a sadistic killer, who worked for Saddam Hussein's Directorate 4. A murderous group who took pleasure in the death of others!' she looked to make sure he'd grasped the seriousness of her words 'Not only is he a very dangerous person now, but some of the crimes he committed against Jewish families in the past, make him one of Israel's *'Ambokshim Biothr'* … 'Most Wanted' to you' she looked around 'It is because you brought him to our attention, that we came to deal with him regardless of what other information you might have. In fact, we formulated a plan of action as soon as we received his photograph on the twelfth, she held up her palm to pre-empt his enquiry 'But, and I mean this, we are also taking your information very seriously'

'Go on, I still don't get why the Brits and Yanks would involve him'

The woman looked at her companion again and nodded in silent agreement 'We have a theory, you said you were involved with the Iranian army prior to the revolution, is that correct?'

'That's right, the Guard de Javadan, but only in a technical capacity'

'It makes sense, Hashimi's father was a colonel in the same regiment 'The Immortals' and was killed by the rebels in the uprising' she could see understanding slowly dawning on him 'And whilst he has no love for the current regime, he is fiercely loyal to his birth country ... do you see where this is going Mr Lamb?' she waited for a response but he merely looked skywards in obvious comprehension. 'So, they certainly wouldn't tell him about the missile plot against Iran... however ... he could have been spun a tale about your involvement back then ... and if so, his agenda is personal ... and lethal!'

He saw it all now 'And it would hide the American and British involvement in my death!' Lamb studied the table top for a second then looked up at the two Israeli's, his mouth firm and his eyes steely. 'I contacted you because I suspected I wouldn't have the skills to deal with him and it seems I was right, so tell me of your plans'

She smiled 'It is extremely rare Mr Lamb, for us to discuss the details of that side of our operations, with someone outside of our organisation'. Sensing his protest she continued, 'However, because of the seriousness of your information and my own assessment of yourself, I have been given permission to fully involve you in our solution' she could see he was pleased 'You should be aware that whilst the four of us only arrived in Nerja yesterday, some of our other colleagues came here in advance. They have not only located him, but have already devised a plan to deal with him. However, I can see where you might fit into it perfectly' she shrugged 'The American we knew nothing about, so that will be a case of observing caution until the Iranian is neutralized. After that we'll see what we can do' she looked around 'Now before we get back to the 'Bikini Project' where you have certain ambitions I believe, we should go over our plans for this evening, in which you Martin Lamb have a walk on part'

Let loose the dogs of war!

***

Mr Churchill was sitting at his desk with his head in his hands 'For god's sake' his whole body shuddered 'Jesus Christ what a bloody mess' despair consumed his mind and indigestion played havoc with his stomach.

266

He'd just gotten off the phone to Pontin, apparently the Spanish Police had contacted the UK's Border Force asking for a passport check. It seems there had been some sort of firefight with a couple of British drug dealers, one had died and the other might never regain his speech. Of course, the Spanish had been informed that the passports were forged, but now the names of the two men were sitting on Pontin's desk. It was the last thing Mr Churchill wanted to hear; the knots of secrecy were unravelling around him!

Sweating, he picked up the red phone 'Hello Mr Lincoln how is the weather your end?'

Whatever the reply, it was about to get stormy!

***

Albazi Hashimi was almost happy, although by most people's standards that was a very loose description. The funeral service wouldn't be held until 7pm this evening and he felt sure Lamb wouldn't turn up much before then. His priority for the latter part of the afternoon, was to line up a female companion for 'after work'. In the meantime, he'd make do with a brandy or two and take advantage of the fine seafood, served outside in the immaculate surroundings of the Marlin restaurant.

Lamb appeared just after 6pm. He was wearing black slacks, white short sleeved shirt and a loosely tied black tie that made him look uncomfortable in the heat. Hashimi observed him joining Sergio's family at the restaurant and correctly assumed, that the priest with them, was going to perform some sort of memorial service inside.

One hour later, everyone vacated the building, then stood around reminiscing themselves into tears about Sergio's good old days. Hashimi took a sip of his fourth Brandy and smiled inwardly, his enemy was within reach. Now, all he needed to do, was destroy him! Afterwards he would enjoy a last night of drunken debauchery. His mind was mulling over the sordid details, when Lamb bid his farewells to the family and solemnly walked past him towards Los Huertos. He appeared to have consumed his fair share of alcohol and seemed faintly unaware of his surroundings. This was too good to an opportunity to miss! Paying his bill, Hashimi followed his prey, along the street in the direction of the Rack and Ruin bar.

When he'd almost reached the bar, Lamb unsteadily turned left and entered the narrow alleyway that lead to the carpark. The manoeuvre didn't alarm Hashimi as he already knew this to be a shortcut down to Calle Carabeo. In fact, it worked in his favour. He paused to allow Lamb time to clear the end of the alleyway, then cautiously crept forward reaching for his gun as he went. Exiting the alleyway, he saw Lamb walk towards two large motor homes, then casually glance around and stop to relieve himself between them.

Realizing that a chance like this was unlikely to present itself again. Albazi Hashimi chambered a round, flicked off the safety and closed in on the static figure of Martin Lamb.

Lynden Harkant casually strolled over Plaza del Olvido just prior to Lamb entering the Quixote bar. He then chose a table inside the Marlin restaurant from where he could observe both the bar and the Iranian. When Lamb later emerged and Hashimi followed him out onto Los Huertos, he in turn followed them both. He only deviated when they cut through the alleyway, he chose instead to enter the Rack and Ruin bar. Once inside he made straight for the rear exit and the steps leading down onto the carpark. He was just in time to see Lamb approaching the motor homes. Followed seconds later by the Iranian, gun in hand.

Not wishing to be deprived of vengeance, he waited until both men were unsighted and then hastily crossed the carpark to come up in front of Lamb and his potential assassin.

As he got near to the front of the first motor home, he withdrew his 9mm Sig Sauer, screwed on the suppressor and rounded the corner ready to fire!

Retribution spun a coin ... heads or tails?

***

Two dramatic incidents occurred on Nerja's main carpark during the late evening of Saturday 14th May 2016

Both were as a direct consequence of the 'Bikini Project'

The first incident was someone placing a gun to the side of Albazi Hashimi's head, whilst at the same time plunging a needle into his left arm, rendering him both dizzy and compliant.

He offered no resistance when his weapon was taken from him ...

and fired!

The second incident was a Soviet made bullet slamming into Lynden Harkant's chest, throwing him violently backwards. It punctured his heart and killed him instantly! He lay face up, his lifeless eyes wide open as if raging at a heaven that would forever deny him entry.

Whilst the gun that killed him disappeared, his own weapon along with the spent shell casing from the uniquely quietened Russian gun, was left where it fell, in the dust.

This was not an oversight!

Following the second incident Hashimi's unconscious body was bound and gagged before being concealed beneath a bed in one of the motor homes. Both vehicles then discretely made their way out of Nerja before heading in separate directions.

Two days later, the Iranian's now lifeless body, would wash-up on an isolated beach some 70 kilometres south. Fingerprints and DNA, taken from the discarded shell casing found on the carpark, would match those of the drowned corpse. Further proof, should it be needed, was the unspent bullet of the same type found in the man's pocket.

***

When releasing the verdict on the dead American Harkant, the Coroner's department in Malaga Province would declare a somewhat vague conclusion:

'That he was the victim of a Targeted assassination by an unidentified person of Middle Eastern origin'

They would also now link it to an incendiary death eight days previously in a Jeep in the mountains above Marbella. That person was also a so-called American lawyer, who had arrived in Spain on the same flight. He was also found to be in possession of an American 9mm pistol and silencer of a similar spec to the one found near the Nerja body.

Coincidentally, both had false passports and neither could be positively identified by the US Department of State or the Bureau of Consular Affairs

They didn't exist!

Subsequent police enquiries would yield no further information on the Nerja incident. In contrast, the country's intelligence agencies, quietly theorized that foreign agents may have played out a covert cleansing operation on Spanish soil. This was bourne out by the players involved and the specialist nature of their weapons.

To placate an enquiring media, the authorities touted another version. Citing the dramatic events in the hills above Puerto Banus, where two Englishmen had also died in a shootout with the Guardia Civil. It was implied that a drug related turf war had taken place, with the inevitable fatalities that brings

.

'All enquiries were now closed, as no further incidents were expected'!

*****

The Israeli 'Kidon' team had planned their mission well … *or so they thought!*

When Hashimi had followed Lamb down Calle Los Huertos, he hadn't noticed the young couple holding hands whilst reading the menu at La Joya restaurant. Neither did he notice them, as they crossed over and followed him past 'Murphy's' Sports Bar and up to Sevillano's restaurant.

Even if he had noticed them, he wouldn't have seen them communicating through their concealed microphones. They used a ploy honed by the 'Mossad' many years previously. Turning to face each other in feigned embrace, they used the other person's tiny radio transmitter, implanted in the collars of their respective tops. To onlookers they were merely whispering endearments, there was none of the comical 'talking into wristwatches. The couple maintained a flow of updates to their colleagues in the motor homes.

Although they saw Lyndon Harkant, he was unknown to them and they wrongly dismissed him, as just another customer of R & R.

It was only when they reached the exit of the alleyway, onto the carpark, that the woman noticed the shadowy figure of a man. He was making his way from the direction of R & R's rear steps, across the uneven ground, towards the front of the nearest motor home.

She also noticed him screwing a silencer on to the barrel of an automatic pistol!

Hashimi was now feet away from his swaying target and raised his weapon to fire into the back of Lamb's head.

The whispered voice came at exactly the same time as the barrel of a gun pressed painfully against Hashimi's temple 'Stay very still and lower your gun'. Next, he felt the sting of a needle in his left arm and his world went blurred. He had no control as the gun was taken from him and firm hands lowered him gently towards the ground. Although incapacitated by the drugs he still thought he heard an urgent shout, followed by the soft 'phutt' of a suppressed shot.

He wasn't wrong! What he heard was Lamb's reaction to a male agent who repeated the curt but precise warning transmitted by his female colleague!

'Male, Armed, Front, Now!'

Harkant fell backwards in death as Lamb spun round and fired in one smooth movement using the gun, he'd just taken off Hashimi.

The Kidon team had come perilously close to failure!

***

Day 19 … Sunday 15th May 2016

An offer he couldn't refuse!

Lamb hitched a ride with the Israeli woman and her three companions as far as the El Inginio shopping centre, Torre del Mar. They pulled off the motorway for a short stop and he gave her the last of his copied sd cards, ignoring her demands for the original. She soon realised it just wasn't going to happen, and was eventually placated with his promise to make it available, should the need ever arise. She understood his reasoning and didn't pursue the subject any further. They thought it amusing when he handed her his tiny knife so she could conceal the card inside the hem of her shorts. However, in terms of world peace and lives in danger, the sd card was currently one of the most valuable items on earth.

Hiding it inside a female Mossad agent's pants was about as secure as you could get!

They sat on the vehicle steps ignoring the drumming of the traffic on the nearby motorway and he told her what had happened to the shirts.

'Were you affected by the deaths?' she asked him.

He replied solemnly 'No, not at all, they killed for two reasons, pleasure and reward! Who' didn't matter to them, neither did Why', afterwards they'd just kill more anyway, so the world was best rid of them!'

She sensed his anger and silently mourned the loss of a once gentle Lamb. His previous emotions had been replaced by icy indifference. What memories of love he once had were now buried in the darkest dungeons of his heart!

She also knew, that despite the previous carnage ... this decent man was the biggest casualty!

Two hours later, he waved the Israelis off and walked towards Billy and Frankie, standing by the Range Rover ready to take him wherever he wished,

Frankie was the first to speak 'You okay Lamby?'

He nodded and cast a last glance at the departing Motorhome 'Yeah I'm okay, I could do with a drink though'

Neither man questioned him about the events in Nerja, he would tell them when he was good and ready.

Billy turned to Frankie 'Tell him about your proposal Frankie, the one we discussed on our way here'

'Yeah why not' he took a deep breath 'It seems to me and Billy that you have nowhere to live … eh … er … Martin?' it came out awkwardly and Lamb smiled 'So we thought … that's me n' Billy here … why not come and live at the villa with us, after all you've already got a room there … and' he paused 'And you obviously like my gin … and … you don't even have to have cucumber if you don't want it' he looked at Billy to cover his embarrassment 'For Christ sake Billy help me out here'

'What Frankie means is …'

Lamb stopped him 'I know what he means Billy' he turned to look at his friend 'Frankie, very soon you'll be going back to London with Betty … trust me, it's all arranged' he patted him on the shoulder 'When you return, I'll be at the villa with Billy, waiting' he looked downwards 'Anyway … I actually like cucumber … I just hate those bloody straws'

No-one else spoke as they climbed into the 4 x 4.

***

The Mouse Roared!

Mr Lincoln was fuming and as usual Mr
Churchill was on the receiving end 'Yes Mr Lincoln,
of course I understand what you're saying, this Lamb
fellow made a fool of us too' he listened incredulously
'No, just because he's British doesn't make it our
fault' he cut through the other man's tirade 'Well you
implied that your men were the best there is … he took
care of them though, didn't he!' point scored, he
continued 'You're not the only one who's pissed off
you know!' the rant kept coming 'Well that's just not
going to happen!' he'd cut across the caller again 'Mr
Lincoln, at what point does it all this end? … for
Christ's sake! … what's next? … a Carrier Group? …
B52 Bombers? … '

The call was suddenly interrupted by a buzzer
on his desk 'Just one second Mr Lincoln'

Impatiently, he crossed the room and opened
the door 'Yes, what is it?' he knew it must be
important, as only the most urgent situations merited
disturbing him in his secure room. However, what his
secretary told him next sent a cold shiver down his
spine;

'Are you sure? … The Israeli Prime Minister is
demanding an immediate meeting? … immediate? …
demanding?'

Three thousand six hundred and sixty-three miles away, an astonished Mr Lincoln was being given the exact same message!

'You go tell that goddam Jewish ... what do ya mean he's already on the line ...!'

Fate finally collided with retribution and all hell Danced!

******

Conclusion;

- The British government granted Frankie the right to return to the UK following pressure from three sources;
  - A front-page story in the Tabloids. detailing the former gangster's help, in bringing down a large drug cartel ... (the author remains anonymous).
  - A polite request, from the Spanish Government, as a reward for his honesty and courage.
  - An uncompromising demand, from the Israeli Knessett.

- Following Betty's return from Tommy's funeral, both her and Frankie eventually departed for London together. She passed away peacefully on Tuesday 30th August 2016, in the little bungalow they bought in the district of Stratford. She was given a traditional East End funeral, with 6 decorated black horses, drawing a glass sided hearse. The church was packed and hundreds lined the route, such was their respect for her lifelong support of Frankie 'The Diamond' Lane.

- Frankie 'The Diamond' Lane returned to his villa in Spain, hollow and distraught. Slowly, Billy and Lamb brought humour and interest back into his life. Quaffing Hendricks, ice and cucumber, but no straws, he enjoyed the banter when all three watched English football on TV, though as a one-time fan of 'The Hammers' he never could get his head around Lamby's support for Liverpool FC.

- Billy 'The Fixer' Cooper has been helping Frankie for forty-two years, since doing jail time together in 1974. He can think of nothing else he'd rather do. Having spent his early years in and out of prison, he found a purpose in life when he met Frankie and Betty and would willingly lay down his life for both. At Betty's funeral he wore a full-dress kilt … for the first and only time in his life.

- Jocelyne (Jocie) Bell wrote her story (anonymously) then returned to her projects' in the UK. She is currently in talks with an American millionaire who wishes to purchase some shares in the 'London Eye'. Her and Billy frequently phone each other, though romance eludes them. Even ignoring the age difference, his commitment to 'The Boss' is absolute. She does though visit 'her Lads' whenever she can.

- **I**srael, demanded an immediate meeting with the US and UK governments, under the guise of talks about the West Bank and Golan Heights. After showing them the recently acquired evidence' an agreement was reached. The US would supply the equipment and technology to build 'Archangel' an anti-ballistic missile defence shield, based on America's 'Patriot' system.

  The UK also reached an agreement, to provide the latest IT Technology to assist in Israel's 'Cyber Intelligence Programme'.

- **T**he 'Compliant but Regretful' Mr Churchill, resigned his post in order to spend more time with his family. His temperament though, had become unpredictable at best and he was eventually divorced by his long-suffering wife, Angela. What really hurt him though, was that she eventually moved in with the portly shadow home-secretary. His indigestion and cholesterol level continue to be a source of irritation to this day.

- **T**he 'Compliant but Arrogant' Mr Lincoln, remained at his post. He continued to rant at other world leaders whenever the opportunity presented itself. Never having been extended the courtesy of a state visit to the UK, he once stated 'Who wants to go to a goddam country that names a ship 'Mayflower' for Christ sake'

- The young Israeli couple Romi Kadosh and Shimon Stern made a short stopover in Athens on their return journey. There, they swapped back the false Belgian ID's and luggage for their Israeli ones.

- Likewise, Shizaf Levi and Alon Dayon retrieved their Israeli ID's on returning their motorhome and 'equipment' to Madrid.

- Martin Lamb 'The Angry Man' couldn't bring himself to attend Betty's funeral. Instead, on that day, he stood on the terrace overlooking the town, and thought of both Mary and her.

  He took a large sip of his Cutty Sark, then raised his glass in a toast 'Mary, I hope your White Rat made you proud' he took another sip 'And Betty, no harm will come to Frankie, I will keep my promise' he paused in reflection, before making his final toast 'Sergio, my friend, the sardines were good, you sleep soundly now' then after swallowing the remainder of his Whiskey, he threw the empty glass over the balustrade ... it was time to get on with life!

It should have ended there … but it didn't …

Friday … November 10th 2017

Unto men there came an Angel

On a chilly winter's morning under an overcast sky, Alonso, the duty manager of the luxurious **Adriana Beach Club Hotel** in Vilamoura Portugal, watched as five men left the warm comfort of a dark blue 4 x 4, and entered the ornate reception area. Two men of eastern Mediterranean appearance, dressed entirely in black and wearing sunglasses, rejected the first suite offered and demanded another random one with unoccupied rooms on either side. Whilst Mr Raphael, Mr Michael and the new man, Mr Uriel signed the hotel register, the two 'men in black' scanned all three rooms for electronic listening devices …

The three VIP's had a highly secret agenda to discuss. Its title was 'The Gabriel Files' … its purpose; to map out the creation and inception of a secret weapons system called 'Archangel'

'! A Agorel Hatnoa'

Saturday … June 23rd 2018

Till death do us part!

'**P**ontin' aka ex-Etonian Tobias Julian Moffat, had been demoted when 'Core Logistical Analytics' was disbanded, shortly after the 'Bikini Project' fiasco'. He'd also been extremely vocal in his resentment of his superiors. They'd accused him of being 'Largely responsible for the failure …

'It was on his watch!'

However, he was now enjoying one of his favourite pastimes: Snorkelling in the sparkling blue Mediterranean waters, off the coast of Rhodes. He was in the picturesque whitewashed resort of Kallithea Springs, the one-time favourite haunt of film stars. The wedding of Stephanie his youngest daughter, had been held in the stunningly beautiful chapel and despite his wife's constant fretting, had gone without a hitch. Now the guests were either swimming, sunbathing or simply quaffing the abundance of free Champagne he'd provided, everyone was relaxed.

Therefore, he wasn't overly concerned, when hands gripped his legs, pulling him down below the surface. It was just a couple of his friends larking about.

The alarm bells only sounded when he looked down and saw two strange men with scuba tanks.

Panicking, he struggled to free himself but the snorkel tube was torn from his mouth and the last of his breath exploded from his bursting lungs. The knowledge that he was about to die, came in a sudden violent moment of terror and disappointment. His last sight, was of the sunlight dancing on the surface ripples five metres above his head. His last thought, was of the pain in his right foot, as it was cruelly jammed into a crevice in the volcanic rock of the seabed.

The two submerged divers, both wearing LAR5010 re-breather tanks, so as not to have air bubbles give their presence away, hugged the cliff wall. They then made their way unseen around the rocky outcrop and pushed out seaward whilst still below the surface. Laying at anchor, one hundred metres away was an inconspicuous white motor launch. After swimming under the boat, to surface on the starboard side, they were helped on board by the third member of the team. The launch, piloted by the fourth then slowly cruised away, un-noticed by anyone on land. The three men and one woman comprising the coldly efficient hit squad, would be well away from the island, before the 'tragic accident' unfolded.

Stephanie Emilia Hansworth (nee Moffat), 23 years old and newly married to Clive had returned to the hotel with her sister Nichola to change out of her wedding dress and prepare for the forthcoming evening meal and celebrations. As they was passing the open door of their parent's suite, she noticed on the coffee table, her father's Samsung and next to it a loose micro-sd memory card.

Eager to see pictures of the wedding ceremony that he had taken, she inserted it into her own phone and opened the gallery.

Fate held its breath!

***

Acknowledgements:

There are many people to whom I owe my gratitude for their support and encouragement, for without it the book wouldn't have been written;

Of course, my wife Carole, who patiently kept silent whilst I laboured away but who was also vocal in praise of my efforts. She also spent many hours with me, proof-reading this book … so if there are still mistakes, it is purely because I wasn't paying attention … thank you darling xxx

My Grandchildren Charlie and Taylor for inspiration and a great Pen-name … xxx

My Son & Daughters and their Families, to whom. I promised a book … I'll let you be the judges.

Sheila, who gave me invaluable advice during her 'Writing Course' thankyou

Thank you to all my friends, who constantly enquired as to my progress, whilst knowing it would also drive me onwards to finish the book, below are a few of their names;

Alan & Rita (I)
Alan & Rita (L)
Adrian & Peter
Morley
Jim & Helen
Big Mick
Mike
Pat & Len
Barber John
Malcolm and Terri
Steve & Carole
Colin & Denise
Heather & Mike
Cath & Paul
John K
Iain & Shireen
Lucille
Tudor & Val
Don & Jackie
Martin & Ger
Linda

If I have failed to mention someone I should have, I apologise wholeheartedly. It is due to my human frailty and can thus be remedied by berating me over a nice cold glass of Chardonnay, at a time and place of your choosing.

Disclaimers;

- Although this book is a work of fiction, for geographical realism, most of the establishments referred to are real. However, please note; other than as a customer I have no commercial connection with these businesses. They are either; very enjoyable places I have frequented with my wife and friends, or highly recommended by those who have left reviews.

- Apart from those who have given their permission to be mentioned. The rest of the characters portrayed in this book are purely fictitious, any resemblance to living or deceased persons is entirely co-incidental.

- To any person who might be of the mistaken opinion that the events in this story are real. May I recommend that you maintain your balance of gin and tonic, you are obviously enjoying life already!

Charlie Taylor

Charlietaylor2397@gmail.com

Forthcoming titles by the same author; 'WMD' the Peacock Brief

amazon.com/author/taylorcharlie2019

Printed in Poland
by Amazon Fulfillment
Poland Sp. z o.o., Wrocław

63078476R00163